The national bestselling author of the Seaside Knitters mysteries returns to find the Crestwood Quilters on pins and needles when a killer strikes...

As owners of the popular bistro The French Quarter, former New York City restaurateurs Jacques and Laurel St. Pierre are the toast of the town of Crestwood, Kansas. Chef Jacques's culinary creations delight the women of the quilting club, who have embraced him as a friend. But Laurel's anti-social behavior confuses Kate Simpson—until she spots Mrs. St. Pierre with another man in what appears to be a lover's spat.

Gossip travels fast in a small town like Crestwood, and rumor has it this isn't Laurel's first indiscretion. She also filed a police report accusing Jacques of domestic abuse. And when Laurel's murdered body is found Jacques is the prime suspect. To prove their friend's innocence, Kate and the Crestwood Quilters must uncover the secrets of Laurel's past—a patchwork history wrapped up in Kate's own teenage years . . .

Books by Sally Goldenbaum

Queen Bees Quilt Shop Mysteries:
A Patchwork of Clues
A Thread of Darkness

Seaside Knitters Society Mysteries:
Murder Wears Mittens
How to Knit a Murder

A Thread of Darkness

Sally Goldenbaum

LYRICAL UNDERGROUND
Kensington Publishing Corp.
www.kensingtonbooks.com

LYRICAL UNDERGROUND BOOKS are published by
Kensington Publishing Corp.
119 West 40th Street
New York, NY 10018

All Kensington titles, imprints, and distributed lines are available at special quantity discounts for bulk purchases for sales promotion, premiums, fund-raising, educational, or institutional use.

Special book excerpts or customized printings can also be created to fit specific needs. For details, write or phone the office of the Kensington Sales Manager: Kensington Publishing Corp., 119 West 40th Street, New York, NY 10018. Attn. Sales Department. Phone: 1-800-221-2647.

Lyrical Underground and Lyrical Underground logo Reg. US Pat. & TM Off.

First Electronic Edition: July 2019
eISBN-13: 978-1-5161-0907-4
eISBN-10: 1-5161-0907-4

First Print Edition: July 2019
ISBN-13: 978-1-5161-0908-1
ISBN-10: 1-5161-0908-2

Printed in the United States of America

The Crestwood Quilters:

Portia (Po) Paltrow: founder and nurturer of the quilting group

Phoebe Mellon: young mother of eleven-month-old twins

Kate Simpson: part-time graduate student

Eleanor Canterbury: heir to the Canterbury family fortune

Leah Sarandon: professor of women's studies at Canterbury College

Selma Parker: owner of Parker's Dry Goods Store

Maggie Helmers: Crestwood veterinarian

Susan Miller: shop manager

Prologue

The tangle of branches made it difficult to maneuver the path. Nevertheless, it was a good choice for the meeting, well hidden from the bridge that spanned the Emerald River. A private place. Few joggers ran on the rutted path, choosing the east side of the river where recently paved paths, well-lit and smooth, ensured more safety.

This route led down to the water's edge, nearly hidden in the curve of sandbar willows and sumac bushes. A better spot to talk. To settle things and clear the air. And then they'd be able to move ahead to a productive and important life. How easy it could be to snuff out that life—those dreams and hopes—with careless words. Everything lost. People hurt. And for what? Why?

A spring moon hung low in the sky, partially hidden by a parade of gauzy clouds that drifted by. Pale light fell through the bridge railing and down to the moving river, roused to life by the wind, its miniature waves slapping rhythmically against the shore.

The forested incline protected walkers and runners from the sounds of the city, muting them and creating a faraway world. All that was real was the river and the sky—and the crunch of gravel just a few feet away.

At first the sound was jarring. But in a split second, calm returned and drove the fear away.

Finally, there'd be resolution. And then it would be over and life would go on.

Bouillabaisse a noble dish is,
A sort of soup or broth, or brew,
Or hotchpotch of all sorts of fishes,
That Greenwich never could outdo.
—W. M. Thackeray

Chapter 1

"Jacques, you've outdone yourself."

Po Paltrow dropped her white napkin beside the plate and looked up into the chef's beaming face. His round knob of nose, slightly out of proportion to his face, was perilously close to her own. Po pushed back slightly in her chair.

"It is my Mama's recipe," Jacques St. Pierre said proudly.

"I had fish tacos once, never fish soup. This is very cool. Like who would have thought?" Phoebe Mellon, a diminutive mother of toddler twins, lifted up from her chair and planted a quick kiss on Jacques's sweaty cheek.

"Bouillabaisse," Jacques corrected, clearly pleased at the attention. His fingers squeezed together and pulled the syllables from his lips like a string of molasses. "Boo-yeh-baze, mon ami."

"Bouillabaisse," Phoebe repeated. "Cool." She headed off toward the ladies' room and a quick cell phone call to check on husband Jimmy and her toddler twins.

"It's quite a feat to make good bouillabaisse in the heart of Kansas," Eleanor Canterbury said. She wiped a trace of soup from the corner of her mouth with her napkin. "But you've done it, indeed, dear Jacques." In her eighty-two years of living life to the fullest, Eleanor had traveled the world several times and eaten bouillabaisse in every coastal village in France. She declared Jacques's among the best, the blend of saffron, orange zest, and crushed fennel seeds balanced perfectly. "Even Venus would be proud," she said.

"Venus who? Venus the goddess?" Kate Simpson lifted her head from scooping up the last tablespoon of soup from her bowl.

Eleanor nodded, poking a loose pearl comb back into her poufy sweep of silvery hair. "It's said Venus served bouillabaisse to her husband, Vulcan, to lull him to sleep while she consorted with Mars." She smiled up at Jacques. "Your soup has a rich history, mon ami."

For an instant, the proud smile slipped from Jacques's face. His smooth pink brow pulled together in a grimace.

"Are you all right?" Po asked.

Jacques gripped the back of Phoebe's empty chair and pushed a smile back into place. "I am excellent," he said. "Just like my bouillabaisse."

"So, tell us your secret," Po said.

"I am happy to share." The small chef leaned over slightly as if keeping his words from the other diners. "My fish is flown in fresh on Mondays, Wednesdays, and Fridays. And those are the only days you will see bouillabaisse on my menu. Never," he wagged his index fingers in the air, "never, ever a Tuesday or a Thursday. The fish need to jump from the packed ice right into my pot. My fennel is fresh, plucked from my own garden. And a touch of pernod, mes amis. Just a touch."

Kate took a hunk of French bread from the basket and wiped the bottom of the blue bowl. A tiny strand of saffron clung to the bread. She looked around the table, her eyebrows arched. "How many pounds do you think we've collectively gained since Jacques came into our lives?"

"Horrible thought," Maggie Helmers groaned, pushing away her plate. "Jacques, you're killing us with this fancy French food." But the look of delight on the veterinarian's face indicated she wasn't about to stop any time soon.

Jacques beamed. The French Quarter, his tiny French bistro, had filled the once-empty storefront on Elderberry Road for a scant six months, but it was lively and thriving, a favorite neighborhood spot, and the Crestwood quilters occupied the round white-clothed table in the back corner far more often than they cared to admit. The small eatery with its tile floor, tightly packed tables, and old framed photographs of the French countryside on the walls had been woven into their lives effortlessly. And they were equally fond of the small round Frenchman who had become a friend.

"We're really here on business. Justification for our decadence," Leah Sarandon said. She smiled up at Jacques. A professor at nearby Canterbury College, Leah was a dedicated member of the quilting group. "We're here to talk about the quilt we're making for you, sweet man. We picked Wednesday night because we thought the place would be empty but look at it—" She gestured to a packed room. "Nearly every table filled."

The Frenchman stepped back and followed her look. A thick oak bar curved along the east wall. The bistro had become a gathering place for drinks after work, a cozy alternative to the downtown bars, and even in the middle of the week it was crowded, people squeezed between the tall stools, raising steins of beer and glasses of Jacques's French wines. Several tall tables near the bar were also filled. Noisy and slightly raucous, just the way Jacques liked it. He nodded to the mayor sitting at one of the small tables. And nearby, Max Elliott, his lawyer and friend, chatted with the president of Canterbury College over a plate of his special escargot. He was glad to see Max back in the restaurant. The last time he had come in for dinner, a young waiter, Randy Haynes, had dumped a plate of wild mushroom fricassee directly onto his lap. Jacques's wife, Laurel, had been standing directly behind Randy, and he suspected her presence had unnerved the young man. He had a wild crush on Laurel; at least that was Jacques's interpretation of the way he stumbled over his words whenever Laurel was near. But Max had been a good sport about the mess in his lap and even refused the offer to pay for the cleaning.

Jacques brought his thoughts back to the table. "It's a good evening," he said.

Po smiled. "It's good for you, good for the Elderberry neighborhood, and certainly good for us."

Phoebe returned to the table and flopped down in her chair. "My Jimmy is beginning to wonder if you have some secret hold on me, Jacques. I think he's jealous."

Jacques threw up his chubby hands in mock horror. "Do not let me be the cause of marital discord, sweet Phoebe."

"Marital discord?" Laurel St. Pierre walked over to Jacques's side and rested one elegant hand on her husband's round shoulder. Laurel was a perfect long-stemmed rose to her husband's daisy. Silky red hair swept her slender shoulders, and her graceful body rose several inches above Jacques's portly frame. Extravagantly high, narrow heels, accentuated her height.

"Well, certainly not yours, Laurel," Po said. She smiled at the lovely hostess.

"Certainly not," Laurel said.

The smile that followed her words was distracted, and Po wondered briefly if Laurel was feeling all right. She watched the hostess's eyes moving over the crowded restaurant, taking in the two couples at the next table, a family back in the corner, the bar tables of business people relaxing with a Scotch and soda before heading home. Watching for anything that needed attention. What an asset she was to Jacques, Po thought.

Her gaze seemed to rest on Max Elliott, a frown marring her smooth forehead. Perhaps she was remembering the awkward spill. Max had told her about it recently, emphasizing the humor in the incident. But then he'd said something curious, something that sounded like the spill might not have been completely an accident.

Laurel focused back on their table when Eleanor asked her if she would like to join them for a few minutes and rest her feet. "I would last two minutes on those heels," she said with a laugh.

"Thank you, Mrs. Canterbury. I'd love to sit with you wonderful women, but we're very busy tonight. I wouldn't want Jacques to fire me." She smiled.

Jacques shook his head. "I tell her not to work so hard. But sometimes she doesn't listen to me."

Laurel smiled at her husband, every bit twenty years her senior, then turned away as Randy walked by, stopping him with a hand on his sleeve and pointing out an empty glass at the next table. Randy's lips opened slightly, his face flushed, and his eyes rested on Laurel for a brief second before he hurried off to do her bidding.

Laurel smiled at the back of his head, then headed toward the hostess station.

"I think Randy Haynes has a crush on your wife," Kate said, nodding toward the blond-headed waiter who was now refilling water glasses at the next table. "I used to babysit for him. He's a sweet kid, though very young and naive."

"He is a good worker. But you are right, Kate. He follows Laurel around like a pup. But then, should he not? She is a beautiful woman. All my helpers here, they think she is so very beautiful, so wonderful."

Kate suspected it was mostly the male helpers, but she kept her words to herself and glanced over at Laurel. Randy had found his way back to the hostess's side, and was happily still as Laurel touched his white jacket, straightening the lapel, and smiling up into his young face. *She's flirting with him.* And then she grimaced, imagining the heartache Randy would suffer digging out from under this crush.

"So, my lovelies," Jacques was saying beside her. "Tell me about my quilt. How is it coming?"

Kate reached into her large purse and pulled out a stack of pictures. She pushed aside the salt and peppershakers and scattered the photos across the empty space in the middle of the table. "Here's my contribution, Jacques. Plump and perfect fish."

Jacques leaned over and looked at the photos, then clapped his hands excitedly. "These are most certainly worthy of my bouillabaisse."

"Thanks. I am a mess in the quilting department, but my camera and I are good friends."

"Kate's photos of the fish are what inspired the design," Susan explained. In addition to helping manage the fabric store, Susan had returned to school herself and was impressing them all with her talent in fiber arts. "The quilt will have an enormous cooking pot at the bottom. These great fish will be reproduced in beautiful colors."

Jacques looked over at a stucco wall, squinting as he imagined the quilting art hanging in that very spot. "Magnifique," he said, his voice hushed as if in a museum.

He turned away briefly as a waiter approached with a question.

"I still think doing an appliquéd quilt is going to drive me to drink," Maggie Helmers said, her plump arms resting on the table edge. Maggie considered quilting her therapy and loved the time away from her veterinary clinic. It refreshed her spirit, she often said. But her skill was limited to backing small shapes with freezer paper, then sewing them up on her mother's old machine. "Those little tiny pieces will make me crazy."

"I understand how you feel, Mags," Leah said. "No worries. You're in charge of background duty. You won't touch a piece of appliqué."

Maggie sighed with relief and looked up as Jacques turned back their way. "So, Jacques, what do you think?" she asked.

The Crestwood quilting group had created more quilts in its thirty-year history than anyone could recollect. Members moved away or died, and daughters or friends were added, but the love and passion for the art was a staple and passed along seamlessly. When Jacques asked for a quilt to hang in his restaurant—a tribute to his mother—they had agreed instantly.

"What do I think?" Jacques beamed in delight. "*Les poisson* will fly across the fabric beneath the magic of your lovely fingers!"

A short distance away, Laurel St. Pierre was once again looking around the room, her clear hazel eyes glancing back into the kitchen through the round window in the door, then to the front door. She held her cell phone in her hand, glancing down at it frequently. She took a slow, deep breath, rotating her narrow shoulders beneath the green silk jacket. She looked again at the group of women sitting across the room. They were gesturing, handing photographs around from one to the other, chatting.

Her eyes narrowed as she stared at Kate, laughing now at something someone had said. *Kate Simpson. Kate.* Laurel felt a painful squeeze across her chest, a tightening rope that made it hard to breathe. She slipped the phone into her pocket and pressed her fingers against her temple, rubbing. The headaches were beginning again. She squeezed her eyes shut, then opened them again, trying to focus on something to alleviate the pain.

Jacques was still at the table, wedged between Kate and Portia Paltrow, leaning over the photographs with a look of utter delight on his plump face. His hair was thinning, visible all the way across the room. Small wisps of brown and gray scattered across the top of his head. Foolish old man, she thought. Boring, silly Frenchman. Laurel brushed her hand across her forehead, staring intently at her husband. She'd actually loved him once. Or had she? He'd certainly been good to her, scooping her up from a dreadful life—a horrible waitressing job in New York and that dreary fourth-floor walk-up. He'd given her a home, more money than she had ever dreamed of, everything she needed to turn herself from a mousy godforsaken creature into Laurel St. Pierre. Sometimes she surprised herself with her elegance. And it brought Jacques great pleasure. He adored her. So much so, in fact, that when she suggested they get away from the city and move to a little Kansas town that he had never heard of, he had agreed. They'd have more time together, she had vowed. And he could create something very special in Crestwood.

He had been so useful to her. So necessary. So compliant.

But those needs were almost nonexistent now. The score was even, or almost so. Soon she would shake herself free and move on. Bury the past forever. Laurel looked again at Jacques and her lips tightened, her head still throbbing with pain. She narrowed her eyes and pressed her lips together until the beauty fell from her face.

Look at you standing there, your forehead sweaty, your tummy bulging beneath that awful apron. The words floated inside Laurel's pained head, an uninvited, disturbing chant. *Oh, Jacques, it would all be easier if you were dead.*

Chapter 2

When Kate and Po left Jacques's bistro a short while later, the sky had darkened, and a crisp breeze stirred the new buds on the trees lining Elderberry Road. Kate looped her arm through Po's and the two walked slowly down the street toward Po's car.

The gesture came more naturally to Kate now than it had a year ago, when she'd returned from California to care for her ailing mother. Somehow, her mother's death had been too connected to Po Paltrow—her mother's best friend and soul mate and a staple in Kate's life from birth. She found her grief turning irrationally to a resentment of her own godmother, this woman who knew her mother even better than she did. At first, she couldn't wait to get back to the life in California, to sell the house her mother had left her and return to her West Coast friends. But it hadn't happened. And now a year later, she couldn't explain it to anyone.

Po turned her head to look at Kate, and thought, as she often did, how proud Liz Simpson would be of her only child. She's decent and kind, Po thought—if a bit unpredictable. And she's totally oblivious to the fact that strangers sometimes stop on the street to look at her, wondering if they've seen her in some romantic comedy with Bradley Cooper or Channing Tatum.

"Why doesn't everyone live in Kansas in the springtime?" Kate said, interrupting Po's thoughts. She looked up at the parade of clouds skittering across the moon. The Big Dipper hung low, nearly close enough to touch, Kate thought. Or to jump right in and take a ride.

Po laughed. "You escaped doing exactly that for several years. And very happily so."

A year ago, Kate would have thought Po's comment a rebuke. But it wasn't, and she knew that. It was a point of fact, and the words were carried on pure affection, along with Po's delight that Kate was there right now. For however long. Kate still insisted she was "just visiting," though no talk of selling the family home ever worked its way into conversation.

"I think I always visited in springtime," Kate answered smugly.

The two women paused in front of Gus Schuette's bookstore, checking out the new books he had placed in his window.

"Well, will you look at Billy McKay," Kate said, pointing to a poster in the back of the window.

Po looked past a display of Ed Bain mysteries to the picture of Bill McKay, a handsome hometown boy who had gone through school with her daughter, Sophie, before going off to Yale. "Billy has certainly made his way in the world, hasn't he?" she said.

MEET THE AUTHOR, the sign read. And below that, the name of Bill's book, and in larger type, CRESTWOOD MAYORAL CANDIDATE.

"Well, he tries." A deep voice answered Po's question, and Kate spun around, nearly landing in the arms of Bill McKay.

"You saying good things about me?" Bill asked, lifting one eyebrow.

Kate laughed. "You're just as conceited as you were in high school, McKay."

"But it looks good on me, right?" Bill shoved his hands in the pockets of his finely tailored pants. "And life itself looks good on you two beautiful ladies. You fine, Po?"

"Doing fine, Billy."

As a youngster, Bill McKay was one of those kids parents liked as much as their kids did. Even when he was in trouble, he'd smile in a disarming way that made you forget he'd chased a ball into your garden, crushing all the new daffodils, or thrown your paper into the birdbath three mornings in a row. Po remembered her daughter Sophie going to a dance with him and being thrilled that the class president had chosen her. And she also remembered Bill being considerate when the high school crush ended. Had they stayed friends? Po couldn't remember.

"So, how lucky can a guy get?" Bill said. He lifted his shoulders, his arms spread wide.

"Probably not much more than this," Kate said. She had been a freshman at Crestwood High when Billy McKay was that senior boy—the football player who drove a fancy car, the guy every girl in the school fell madly in love with. Kate hadn't been impressed back then. Silly crushes. Bill seemed to covet them, which made it worse. Maybe that's why she wasn't impressed. But grown up, he seemed to have a bit more going for him. "So, you wrote a book. Impressive. What's it about?"

"It's kind of an inspirational book for kids," he said. "It's about living in a small town and seeking your dream. Gus here," he nodded toward Schuette's bookstore, "is making more of it than it deserves."

"Well, it sounds like you're doing exactly that, Bill—seeking your dreams," Po said. "I'm sure your parents are proud of you."

For years, Jackson and Florence McKay had lived in Po's comfortable neighborhood, their large, stately brick home known by everyone for its manicured lawn and for the extravagant Halloween treats the owners dished out. Bill's dad, a successful businessman, owned several companies in Crestwood and Kansas City, although word had it that he wasn't always an easy man to work for.

"Sure," Bill said.

"I haven't seen them around the neighborhood lately."

"They're in Florida most of the time, living the good life. Semi-retired, my father says. I'm handling one of the businesses—McKay Commercial Real Estate."

Just then a young woman walked out of the bookstore and over to Bill. She touched his arm lightly, then smiled at Po and Kate.

Bill put out his arm behind her back, pulling her into the group. "Hey, babe, meet two old friends of mine. Po and Kate. This is Janna Hathaway, my fiancée."

"You're engaged?" Kate said. "Congratulations."

Bill laughed. "I know—who'd have thought I'd ever settle down?"

But Kate hadn't wondered about that at all. She was thinking instead of the girls she'd seen at his side when he was determined to be the coolest kid in the school. His girlfriends were always the prettiest and glitziest. Janna Hathaway was neither. Except for her Prada bag and an elegant Italian leather jacket, Janna was plain, the kind of person who could easily get lost in a crowd—her nose long and thin, her pretty eyes too close together, her eyebrows narrow.

Janna moved closer to Bill as he explained to her that he had known Kate in high school and Po had helped him finance his first ten-speed by letting him mow her lawn one summer.

Po asked about the wedding, and Kate half-listened as Janna explained that the preparations were nearly complete even though the wedding wasn't scheduled until the following spring. She and her mother were both planners, she said, and then she described an extravagant wedding that would certainly be the highlight of Crestwood's social season. Bill seemed slightly disinterested in the plans but listened politely as Janna talked, nodding now and then.

"Janna's from St. Louis," Bill said finally, steering the conversation away from cakes and florists and gift bags.

"How did you meet Bill?" Po asked.

"Our fathers, actually. In fact, my father will be doing some business with Bill soon, helping him build his business."

"So you'll live here in Crestwood, then?" Kate asked. And then she laughed at herself. "Duh. Sorry. Of course you'll be living here. Prospective town mayors usually live in their towns."

"I'm building a house on the east side of town," Bill said. "Out past Canterbury College. Janna's here for a few days to work with the interior designers. She's pretty good at that sort of thing."

Janna smiled. "That's what he thinks. My real reason for being here is to find out more about this incredible man I'm about to marry. Kate, you'll have to fill me in on what he was like in high school. Were you friends?"

"No."

"Hey," Bill said, feigning hurt.

Kate ignored him. "Billy was older, for starters. But he was pretty much everyone's friend, at least the way I remember it. I remember that he talked to everyone. Especially around the time of class elections."

Bill laughed. "Well, it worked, didn't it?"

Kate laughed. But it had, she remembered. Bill McKay managed to win every class election, every award, and every girl's heart. She remembered his parents at the honor assemblies, nodding approval in a way that said this was expected of their only son. And so was the college he would attend. When he was accepted at Yale, there was a front-page story in the town newspaper citing his accomplishments.

"It will certainly work this time, too," Janna said, looking over at the poster in the window. "Bill will be an amazing leader. He will put this town on the map. We will make sure it happens."

Bill was still revisiting his high school years. "I talked to you, Kate, I'm sure I did. I even remember a talent show performance you were in with that awful band. Your hair was pink, and you were the star of the show."

Kate laughed hard. "Yeah, I was great."

Janna watched the banter, then shifted her bag from one arm to the other and smiled apologetically at Kate and Po. "I hate to end this reverie, but we should go. Bill and I were about to find a place to eat and it's getting late." She looked up at Bill, her brows lifted, seeking agreement.

"Food? Oh, you need to go to Jacques's," Kate said, the taste of bouillabaisse still on the tip of her tongue. "It's absolutely the best restaurant in Crestwood, bar none."

"See? I told you it looked good, Bill." She turned to Po and Kate. "Bill never eats in a restaurant until it's been operating for a year. It's a McKay rule, he tells me."

"Well, then he's foolish and will miss out on something special," Kate said. Po agreed.

Bill shrugged. "I had my heart set on Mexican tonight," he said to Janna. "That sounds good to me, too," she said immediately.

"I'll take you to France on your honeymoon," Bill added. "Will that make up for it?"

Janna giggled like a schoolgirl. Kate looked at Bill, then Janna. She was a conundrum. Or he was. Or maybe it was the combination. On one hand, Janna seemed to melt in the presence of her fiancé. On the other, she seemed to have some kind of influence on him. Weird. Maybe it was something money did.

Kate was puzzled, then shook it off. *What relationships didn't have some inconsistencies, once you peeled off a layer or two? Most of hers did. The last one certainly did.*

"I guess I'd better go feed my bride-to-be," Bill said. "But it is wonderful to see you two." He smiled warmly at each of them, meeting their eyes directly. Then a friendly nod.

Just like a politician, Kate thought. Then scolded away the thought.

Bill nodded at Gus's poster and then said, as if reading Kate's thoughts, "And hey, your votes would be welcome." He grinned at Kate.

Kate flushed, slightly uncomfortable. "Knowing you, Bill McKay, you'll charm your way to the top, just like Billy the Kid did," she said.

Bill laughed, then turned serious. "I've grown up a little bit, honest. At least I hope I have. I still want your vote, though, but I hope you'll give it to me because I want to do good things for this town." Then, in an instant, the polished smile returned and one arm slipped around Janna's back. With a nod, the would-be mayor turned and walked away, leading his fiancée into the night.

The bookstore door slammed and Gus Schuette walked out, looking after the disappearing couple. "You know he's gonna get it, don't you?" he said.

"You think so?" Po asked.

"No question in my mind. He's seems to have turned into a decent sort."

"You may be right, Gus," Po said.

"I've volunteered to help him out some. Arrange some gatherings, that sort of thing. You think I'd have lassoed the moon for him, all the thanks he's pouring on me." He chuckled.

"That's nice of you, Gus," Po said. And she meant it sincerely. Billy was lucky to have Gus Schuette on his side. He knew everyone in town, and beneath his sometimes-grumpy exterior, he was well respected and smart. "But if push comes to shove, I think you'd make a mighty fine mayor, Gus Schuette."

Gus stood in front of his bookstore, feeling the white light of a brilliant spring moon bathing him in its glow, as if blessing him in some off way. He scratched his chin, tasting the compliment—and liking the flavor.

Hmmm, he thought, turning to inspect his reflection in the glass. *Mayor, eh?*

Chapter 3

"Po, I'm addicted." Kate dropped her backpack on a chair in Po's kitchen and walked toward the refrigerator. She opened the door and peered inside. "All I want to do is take pictures. The heck with grading papers, writing papers, going to school." She pulled out a bottle of water and looked over her shoulder at her godmother.

Po was sitting at the wide wooden table paying bills, her reading glasses balanced on the end of her nose. Spring sunlight poured through the back windows and across the kitchen and family room, highlighting several silvery streaks in Po's shoulder-length hair. She looked over the top of her glasses at Kate. "You're good at it. 'Follow your passion,' your mother would say."

Kate laughed and walked across the kitchen. "*Dreams*, I think she said. But she didn't mean it. She meant the dreams you two thought up and approved of." She pulled out a chair across from Po and sat down, propping her elbows on the thick table.

Po laughed. "Well, maybe. But you have to admit, you had some crazy ideas in your youth."

"Me?" Kate lifted one brow, a smile tugging at her lips, her large brown eyes focused on Po. She no longer had to restrain the automatic response to anything Po—or once upon a time, her mother—said. To dispute their ideas outright. Her mother's illness and dying had had a tempering effect on her need to rebel. That and age, she supposed. Billy McKay claimed he had grown up. Maybe he had. But she definitely had. Becoming an orphan at age thirty had a sobering effect on how one approached life.

"I was a jerk some of the time, back then," she said aloud.

Po laughed, tapped some numbers into her computer, then closed the lid. "Sometimes you were. But we loved you anyway. Your mom never lost hope in you. And as for this new dream, photography might well pass the approval test. It certainly beats following some alternative rock band halfway across the country when you should have been in summer school. You have an eye for photography, Kate. You see things through that lens that I don't see. It amazes me."

Kate smiled, warmed all the way through. Sometimes she amazed herself, she had to admit. She'd let the photos rest a few days, then revisit the shots of a park bench in the fog or the movement of the river on a windy day, and she saw magical things in the shadows and angles of those simple scenes.

She looked over at a pile of fabric on the other end of the table. "You know, Po, I think I'll actually be more successful with this new kind of quilt we're doing for Jacques."

"Because it involves food?"

"Well, that, too," Kate admitted. Her long slender body handled food nicely, distributing it on her lanky frame without ever turning to fat. "I like the appliqué idea. No matter what Maggie says, I think I'll be better at that than trying to line up corners."

"Some quilters like it, some don't. We'll see. It isn't easy."

Kate took an apple from a wooden bowl and rubbed it absentmindedly on her sweatshirt. "Jacques seems thrilled with the whole idea. But did you notice Laurel last night?"

"I did. She seemed worried."

"Or angry. I caught her looking at us once, and there was fire in those gorgeous eyes."

"Hmm. Maybe. Perhaps she thinks we're bad for business, taking up that big round table so often."

"That wouldn't make much sense. It's not like Jacques is feeding us for free."

"True. But she's very involved in the business, Jacques told me. It surprised him when they first moved here, but now he's nothing but proud of her. Maybe you misinterpreted the look."

Kate shrugged. "There's something about her that throws me off kilter. You know that feeling of déjà vu you sometimes get? I swear I've met Laurel St. Pierre before. Is that possible?"

"Jacques said they met on the East Coast. New York, I think. I'm not sure if they've lived in California."

"They haven't. I asked her. She's never been there, and she seemed insulted when I said I thought I knew her from somewhere. She's strange, Po. I think—"

The rattle of the back door stopped Kate's words mid-sentence.

"Hi, beautiful ladies." P.J. Flanigan walked through the kitchen door and across the room. He leaned over Po and planted a kiss on her cheek. A hunk of brown hair fell across his forehead. Then he rounded the table and stood behind Kate. Bending slightly, he whispered into her ear. "Where've you been all my life?"

"Right here. Just waiting. Waiting for Flanigan," Kate answered, moving slightly forward and away from the warm breath much too close to her ear.

"Hmm, catchy title. Think I'll write a play about that."

She twisted her head and looked up at him. "Now back off, Flanigan. I like my space," Kate said.

P.J. lifted one brow. Then he straightened up and headed for Po's collection of coffee mugs hanging on a line of wall hooks. "As lovely as you two are," he said over his shoulder, "I'm here on business." P.J. filled his mug and turned back, leaning against the counter. "We had a strange thing happen last night at the department. I thought maybe you could shed some light on it."

"What's that?" Kate took a bite of her apple and watched P.J. as he helped himself to a muffin from Po's bread container. He was as comfortable in Po's kitchen as she was, maybe more, having known the Paltrows all his life. It was clear that the young lawyer-turned-policeman loved Po—a fact that somehow created other feelings that were beginning to play around inside her when P.J. came into a room. He had grown up to be a nice guy. Maybe even more than that. And she was enjoying hanging out with him, which is how she described their evenings together to Po. And anyone else who asked. Entanglements were something she didn't want in her life right now. But somehow, tangling with P.J. had a pleasant spin to it.

"We had a domestic violence call," P.J. said, scattering Kate's thoughts. "It was from Laurel St. Pierre."

"No!" Kate and Po's voices collided in the kitchen's coffee-scented air.

"Yep. About one a.m. I wasn't there, but Frank Stangel—a buddy—said it was really strange. He took the call, and when he and his partner got to the St. Pierres' place, they found the Mrs. sitting on the front step of the house, crying her eyes out. No bruises, no signs of violence, but the lady was very distraught."

"And Jacques?" Kate asked.

"Nowhere to be found."

"That doesn't make sense, P.J.," Po said. "Jacques is a fine man. And gentle as a lamb. What's more, he adores his wife." But even as she spoke, worry creased her forehead.

"I guess we don't know what goes on behind closed doors," P.J. said. "They were both at the restaurant last night," Po said. She thought back, wondering about the mood of the chef and of his wife. P.J. took a bite of the muffin and washed it down with a swig of coffee. "Did you notice anything strange? The French Quarter is drawing quite a crowd. Maybe they were stressed out and took it out on one another."

Kate and Po were quiet, thinking back to the amazing bouillabaisse and crusty French bread. It was easier—and far more pleasant— to think about food than the observations they'd had about the people who made it and managed the restaurant. It was one thing to gossip among friends, another to lay it all out for a policeman's mind to dissect. Even if that policeman was P.J.

"Laurel…" Kate began cautiously. "Well, she seemed distracted. Something was on her mind."

"Jacques was his usual happy self, and affectionate toward Laurel the way he always is. A little nervous at one point, maybe, but that might have been the crowd, the kitchen help, a dozen things. No, this doesn't make sense." Po shook her head. "Did you ever find Jacques?"

"Yep. Cruiser spotted him walking along the river path about dawn. Had his apron on and all. He said he'd been at the restaurant—"

"In the middle of the night?" Kate asked.

"He said he sometimes does that. He seemed shocked that Laurel had called the police. They'd had an argument, he said, that's all. And he'd gone back to the restaurant to 'cook it off,' as he put it. Then decided to take the long way home to relax himself."

"And?"

"That's it. But Laurel claimed it was way more than an argument, even though no one saw signs to validate her statement. She said she was afraid of him and couldn't we do something?"

"Afraid of Jacques? That's absolutely ridiculous." Po shook her head and pushed her glasses up into her gray-streaked hair. "It's true he hasn't lived here that long, but I know an honest, good person when I see one. I've never been wrong. Jacques is a friend and there is no way he'd have done anything to harm Laurel."

"It's odd, for sure," P.J. said. "I thought he was a nice guy, too. Don't care for that fancy French food much, but he's always happy to make me a steak."

"Such plebian taste," Kate said. "I'm not sure why we let you hang around."

"Boyish charm, I suspect." He grinned at her over his coffee mug.

Po watched the two banter back and forth. Kate was good at pushing people away. She'd even done it with her in her subtle protests of her mother and Po's friendship. She had made it clear she didn't need two mothers. One was sometimes more than enough. Po had learned to give her goddaughter space after she lost her mother. And it seemed to be working.

She wondered if P.J. knew that secret. The attraction was palpable. But it was clear that Kate was resisting, unsure whether she was ready to plant any roots in Crestwood, Kansas. Po would keep her distance, but she'd known them both since they were babies, and she thought Crestwood roots were just fine.

Kate pushed back her chair and stood. "This mess with Jacques upsets me," she said, worry lines returning to her forehead. "There has to be another side to the story." She walked over to the sink.

"There usually is." P.J. took a long swallow of coffee. "Great brew, Po."

"So, what do you do now?" Po asked. "Did Laurel file a report?"

"Yep, she did. But it'd be reported anyway."

"That's crazy," Kate said.

"She wanted to make sure it was in a file somewhere, and it was her right. So now if there's a next time, it will make a difference in how it's looked at. But for the present, it's 'he said, she said.'"

"And she's wrong." Kate rinsed out her mug and put it in the dishwasher.

"Spoken with pure objectivity," P.J. said.

"Intuition," Kate snapped back. "If you think Jacques could ever hurt anyone, P.J. Flanigan, you're dead wrong. He's a prince, like Po said. And you can tell your buddies at the department that."

"Whoa," P.J. said, getting up from the table. "Don't get your dander up, Katie. They're just doing their job."

Kate glared at him, then relaxed slightly. "I suppose." She checked her watch and picked up her backpack, slipping it over one shoulder. "Well, I have a date with a professor to talk about cameras, so I'm out of here. You two have a good day."

Kate blew a kiss across the room, then disappeared out the back door, letting it slam behind her.

"She's an interesting young woman," P.J. said, watching her leave.

Po laughed. "Yes. I guess you could say that."

"But she may be wrong about Jacques, Po. The guys at the station said Laurel St. Pierre was mighty convincing."

"That's too bad, but I think they were fooled, P.J. I don't mean to speak ill of her, but she has a bit of the actress in her."

P.J. shook his head and carried his mug to the sink. "You're as stubborn as Kate is, Po. Just be careful, is all I ask."

"Be careful? P.J., now I think it's you who has the dramatic streak. Be careful of a sweet French chef with a heart as big as his amazing mousse au chocolat? Shame on you."

But after P.J. left, Po sat alone at the kitchen table, her bills in a neat stack next to her laptop, and her mind wandering back over conversations she had with Jacques in recent days. A spring wind had picked up and beat the branches of her willow tree against the side of the house. An uncomfortable beat. One that matched the feelings hammering around inside her.

A chance meeting in the market a few days before had shown her that the French chef wasn't always as cheerful as he appeared in his restaurant. Over bins of fresh produce, he had seemed worried. When she'd asked if everything was all right, he had pushed a smile across his round face and assured her everything was fine. *And if not perfect*, he confided, *that was all right. One could live with small problems. That was life, n'est-ce pas?*

At the time she had assumed it was the stress of running a successful restaurant, keeping staff in line, juggling expenses. Now she wasn't so sure. Jacques said he could live with it.

Live with what? she wondered now

Chapter 4

Kate's camera hung loosely from her neck, moving rhythmically as she jogged slowly along the river path in Riverside Park. The park ran along both sides of the Emerald River, a meandering stretch of water that curved its way through the center of the small hilly town. Wide bridges anchored it at either end, with one in the middle.

The park had been talked about for as long as Kate could remember. Her own father, Jim Simpson, had spearheaded a group of town leaders, forging the way for the acres of green that now hugged the sides of the river.

Dad would have loved this, she thought. Paved paths and gaslights lining the paths along the entire length of the park. Small walking paths spread out from the river like a spider web, meandering back into clumps of trees and picnic tables and play areas with sandboxes and swings. The bridges provided the perfect place to stand and watch small kayaks and paddle boats go up and down the river. In a month, summer concerts would start in the gazebo up near the bridge, and the park would be teeming with residents and college kids, the bridges crowded, the smell of hotdogs, beer, and lemonade filling the air.

But today the park was quiet, with just a smattering of college runners, a few mothers pushing strollers, and some children just out of school chasing a kite up the hill. Kate came to a stop beside a wooden bench, cemented into the cobbled path. She sat down, fingering the Minolta hanging loosely around her neck.

"Hey, Miz Simpson, what's up?"

Kate looked up into the grinning face of Amber King, a student in the senior English class in which Kate often substituted. "Hi, Amber. What are you doing here?"

Amber flopped down on the bench beside her and pointed to her backpack. "I hang out here and people watch. Fodder for my writing." She looked at Kate's camera. "Looks like you do the same. Awesome." Kate lifted the camera up to her eye, focused on Amber, and snapped it a few times. "You're right, we're alike in that way. I see the world and people through this lens—you see them in a whole new way, painting them with words."

Amber liked the description and grinned. "I signed up for your digital class so I'll see twice as much."

"Cool. Sometimes I almost feel like a voyeur, though. Take a look," Kate said.

Amber took the camera and looked through the square viewer. She focused on the river and a family of goslings slowly heading downstream. She shifted sideways on the bench, the camera still in her hands and snapped away at the scene behind her, a young mother and her baby lying on their backs on the side of the hill, and further up, capturing a couple as entwined with one another as the tangled branches behind them.

Kate watched Amber as she pivoted on the bench. She was zooming in on the trees up the hill—or maybe the couple, snapping a sequence of shots like a pro. Kate wondered if she had been that sure of herself at seventeen. The kids she taught fascinated her, and though substitute teaching had never been on her list of things she wanted to do in life, she was discovering that she liked it. The chance opening when she had returned to Crestwood last year had filled a need for both her and the high school. Returning to the same wide halls that housed four years of her life was a nostalgic trip. Some of the teachers who had taught Kate were still there, including Betsy Carroll, a favorite guidance counselor who had spent much of her time keeping Kate on the straight and narrow. She enjoyed the time she spent with Betsy, speaking adult to adult.

And then there were kids like Amber, who made her think she might sign on again next fall if she was still around. She loved her spirit and her sense of self and the pink streak in her hair.

"Very cool camera, Miz Simpson. Digital is the way to go. And the way for me to go is up that hill to ponder the poetry of Yeats." Amber handed the camera back to Kate. "I will leave you alone to your voyeuring. Catch you later."

Kate chuckled and watched Amber saunter up the path until she found a grassy spot beneath a tree and settled down. Kate followed her through the camera's eye, then panned across the hilltop to the couple standing close in the shade of the trees. It was a camera-perfect sight—deep green trees, a textured mulched path, and two entwined figures painted in shadows and lost in a passionate embrace.

She lowered her camera to her lap and squinted at the two figures. There was something oddly familiar in the woman's stance, her hands now on her hips. Kate's eyes focused, the image clearing, and watched as the couple moved apart. *I am a voyeur*, she thought to herself, embarrassed.

But before the couple completely escaped her look, the woman lifted one hand and slapped the man forcefully across the face. In the next instant, they moved through the trees and out of Kate's view.

"Well, I'll be," she murmured. She slipped the camera into a small leather case, strained unsuccessfully to catch another glimpse of the couple, and then turned and headed toward home.

* * * *

"I swear it was Laurel St. Pierre," Kate said. "And she was very, very cozy with some tall, dark stranger. Then all of a sudden, the embrace dissolved and she whacked him one."

Kate sat with Po and Eleanor Canterbury on the Endicott back porch, sipping light gin and tonics in the diminishing daylight. Kate had kept the disturbing scene in the river park to herself for twenty-four hours, but wrapped in a sweater and ensconced in a comfortable porch swing, Kate blurted out what she had seen.

The early-evening cocktail ritual was something Po's friends could count on. In the early years of child rearing, the Endicott porch was a place that neighborhood moms gathered, watching the kids play in the long backyard and relishing the adult discussion. Then in a blink of an eye, those same kids, having switched from apple juice to beers and cocktails, were joining them when home on a vacation.

It had become a quieter gathering for anyone who happened by, sometimes just for the company, and sometimes, like today, to sort through surprising and disheartening news.

"You're absolutely sure it wasn't Jacques with her? He adores that woman," Eleanor asked.

Kate shook her head. "Not a chance. Not unless he has grown a head taller—and lost inches everywhere else."

"Maybe it was an innocent, chance meeting. An old friend. A relative? Or…"

"One wouldn't kiss relatives or casual friends like that—not even ones you really liked." She thought back over the incident, replaying it in her mind: the couple pressed together as if a giant vise had squeezed their bodies tight, and then suddenly arms flailed. She'd been too far away to hear the sound of the smack, but felt sure someone was left with a bruise on his cheek.

"It was definitely not Jacques, but it was difficult to make out definite features because they were standing in shadows. It was the way the woman was standing that first got my attention. The lift of her head. And then, when they turned, a splash of sunlight came through the branches highlighting brilliant streaks of red hair."

"Hmm. Yes, that hair would be difficult to hide." Eleanor said. Her gnarled fingers rested on the arms of a rocking chair, the motion of the chair somehow comforting. Her cane was hooked over the porch railing. Po sometimes worried about Eleanor's evening walks from her home on the edge of the campus and into the tree-lined neighborhood where Po lived, but she insisted that the hand-carved cane she'd picked up at a market in Spain was weapon enough should anyone give her trouble.

"Laurel is a troubled young woman," Eleanor said. "I see pain behind those pretty eyes. I see it sometimes when she's hostessing at the French Quarter. And I saw her at Wally's drugstore one day when I was picking up my vitamins. She was asking Wally about a stronger medication for pain. When I approached her, she told me she had headaches sometimes and said she was going to have her eyes checked." Eleanor rested her silvery coif against the back of the rocker. "Maybe so, but just between the three of us, I think her pain comes from another place."

"Maybe," Kate said. She curled her long legs up onto the swing, wrapping her arms around her knees. "You're a compassionate soul, Eleanor. You are. But frankly, her headaches don't bother me as much as the thought that she might be hurting Jacques. That's who I care about."

"We all do, Kate," Po said. "But what goes on between a couple is their business."

"Oh, phooey, Po. You sound just like my mother. You two spent way too much time together. If Jacques is having trouble, I don't care who it's with, I want to help him. And I don't trust Laurel St. Pierre for a single second." Kate swirled the ice cubes in her glass, the clink sounding loud in the quiet evening air. "There's something about her, I don't know. Like she's looking at me, waiting for me to say something to her. It's strange. And, frankly, I don't want her messing with Jacques's heart."

Po got up and flipped a switch that lit a low row of gaslights bordering the path at the bottom of her porch steps. They flickered on, bright against the darkening night. She paused next to the porch swing and looked down at Kate. "Everything you are saying may be true. Laurel may be hiding some dark secret, she may be having an affair, she may have awful headaches. But the only thing we know for certain is that there's not a thing any of us can do about it."

* * * *

After Kate and Eleanor left, Po went inside and plugged her phone into the speaker. Soon Norah Jones's soft smoky voice filled the room, bringing pleasure along with a nice sense of wakefulness. Po settled down in front of her laptop at the dining table, bringing up a half-finished article she was writing on crazy quilts.

But her thoughts were meandering, scattering the description of a quilt form's utilitarian beginnings, and turning again and again to images of Jacques: Jacques leaning over their table, his smile wide as he told him of plans for his anniversary quilt; Jacques beaming as praises for his entrees echoed throughout the restaurant; Jacques introducing his beautiful wife.

Po forced herself back to the words on the screen—the tale of well-to-do Victorian women piecing together expensive silk and satin fabric pieces as they wiled their casual days away, creating a plethora of colorful parlor hangings. A world apart from that of busy Crestwood moms, running children to school and soccer games, band practice and birthday parties, then rushing off to offices or courtrooms or classrooms.

Or helping husbands manage restaurants.

Laurel had been a part of the French Quarter from its opening months before. Always at Jacques's side, greeting customers. Keeping a watchful eye on everything that went on in the restaurant. Occasionally giving Jacques a hug. A kiss on his cheek.

But things were different, even when they tried to say Jacques was the same sweet man. His ready smile had a droop to it, his chuckle was a little more forced. And even his interest in the quilt they were fashioning for the back wall of his restaurant seemed a little distant, less exuberant. Did this liaison, or whatever it was that Kate thought she saw, have something to do with it?

She needed to take her own advice; there was nothing they could do about it. And even if it weren't intrusive to get involved, she had too many things on her own plate to dive, uninvited, into someone else's personal problems. Po stared at the screen on her computer. What was her business was finishing this article.

She focused in, but the writing came in fits and starts. Finally she gave up, fixing some sleepy-time tea and heading to bed. Somehow she anticipated sleep would be as difficult as the writing had been. She couldn't put her finger on the cause. Concern for Jacques? A writing deadline? Or was it just one of those anxious times in life when things aren't as smooth and tranquil as they sometimes are? Her mother had always told her those were the fruitful, creative times, like a plant beneath the soil's surface, just about to burst forth in brilliant colors. Restlessness could be a good thing, her mother had insisted.

But Po's optimistic and wise mother never mentioned the other side of restlessness. The dark side that might be the harbinger of distressing events.

Her mother would never have imagined—not in a million years—that the nagging unrest that kept her daughter tossing beneath her fine cotton sheets that moonless night might have portended something quite the opposite of new life.

Chapter 5

The next morning came far too early, but a brisk shower brought life back into Po's body. That and the awareness that it was Saturday morning. And Saturday morning meant quilting and friends and talk, no laptops and article notes allowed. She slipped on a pair of light slacks and a cotton blouse and sweater, and packed up her knitting bag. Downstairs, in the kitchen, she stood in a puddle of sunshine and gulped down quickly a glass of orange juice, then moved out into her day.

Spring was everywhere, birds singing from the budding trees, clear morning light slanting through the branches. A season of hope. Po walked into it with quick steps, hoping the crisp air and sunshine would shake away the uneasy vibes that had found their way into her sleep, persistent as fruit flies.

She loved Saturday mornings and was determined not to let unknown anxiety interfere with the day. It had kept her from rising at five for her morning exercise, and that was the extent that she would allow it to ruin her day. Po moved aside while two coeds raced by, long ponytails flying. She smiled at their backs, sensing the welcome release of exam stress as they ran.

The quilters met at Selma's fabric shop every Saturday morning, come tornado or sunshine. Not everyone made it each Saturday, but they'd decided a long time ago that meeting monthly didn't do the trick, especially when they were working on a particular project, like Jacques's wall quilt or pieced blankets for the homeless shelter. Sometimes there would only be three of them on the weekend morning, sometimes six or eight. Po sometimes missed the gathering when her grandchildren and daughter were in town. Or when one of her sons managed a weekend away from his busy life in California. Or if she was giving a Saturday talk.

But the hours spent in Selma's quilting room engaged and refreshed her as few other things did. The familiarity, the peace. The friendships. *Thirty years. Could it be that long?* She had joined the unofficial Queen Bee Quilters as a young bride, and then suddenly, it seemed, she was a young mother, teaching writing and helping her husband, Scott, up the ladder of academia. Eventually, Scott climbed all the way to the top— the youngest president in the history of Canterbury College. And all the while Po was a regular at the Crestwood Quilters gathering.

"You'd like this group, Scott," Po said softly as she sidestepped a child's scooter left out on the sidewalk. Her quilting bag bounced against her hip. "Maggie Helmers—she was in school with Sophie, you remember? She's now Crestwood's busiest veterinarian. There's a young mom—Phoebe— who is married to Jimmy Mellon. You knew his parents. They were big benefactors at the college. A bit stuffy, you used to say, though well intentioned, I suppose. And of course, dear Eleanor Canterbury is still alive and never misses a session—unless she's off on an African safari or visiting Egyptian pyramids. I swear, Scott, at eighty-two she has more wind in her sails than that boat you used to race on Lake Quivira."

Po stopped and leaned over a bed of daffodils at the edge of a neighbor's lawn. *Lovely.* She continued on, picking up her conversation. "And Leah, of course. She still teaches at *your* college—it will always be *your* college. Leah is still giving the male faculty a hard time, still grateful to you for the day you promoted her to department head against the wishes of that stodgy board you had to deal with. Susan Miller is another quilter—you didn't know her—she's a younger woman—well, younger than I, anyway—who helps Selma in the shop. Very creative."

"Who are you talking to?" Kate rode up alongside Po, bringing her bike to a stop and hopping off. "I called to you but you didn't seem to hear. You were deep in conversation."

Po smiled and brushed a loose strand of hair behind her ear. She pushed her sunglasses to the top of her head and looked at Kate. "Yes."

Kate straightened the wheel of her bike and began walking with it alongside Po. "I talk to my mom, too," she said. "We even argue sometimes— just like old times, right? They're still with us, for sure."

Po turned her face and emotion in the other direction and waved at a woman across the street. When she changed the subject, her voice was husky. "You're early for quilting. That's not like you at all."

Kate's laugh, a bit too loud, filled the space between them. "Miracles happen. You're early yourself. Are you hoping Marla has pulled a tray of cinnamon rolls out of the oven?"

"I can smell them. But not today. Maybe a cup of coffee. I didn't sleep well." She rotated her shoulders, shrugging off a cramp. "I thought maybe Selma might need some help getting the store ready. Since she started displaying quilts on Friday nights, she's had a crowd of people going through, and sometimes it's a mess on Saturday morning. The display is great for business but lots of work."

"I like what's she's done. It's a great way to use that long wall. And the quilts she displays are gorgeous. But what we really need is a quilting museum. There's one in San Jose—"

"You visited a quilt museum?"

Po's unaltered surprise brought a laugh from Kate. "Well, okay, so I didn't exactly go in. But I had friends who did. Quilting is even hot in California, you know." She wrinkled her nose at Po. "But maybe I would go in now. Now that I have a better relationship with quilts. But anyway, they—my friends—said it's amazing. Gorgeous, arty quilts made by passionate quilters, just like all of you. We could do that here, have a museum. We have lots of quilters and plenty of passion."

Po held back her smile. She didn't push Kate on the passionate quilters comment. It was at a snail's pace to be sure, but Kate was slowly coming around to enjoying the hobby that her mother had loved. And her mother had a hand in it, in Po's opinion. Kate took the first step the day she discovered her mother's fabrics and quilting supplies in the attic after Liz had died—and had found a bit of her mother in the cotton squares.

"I think Selma and Susan have actually talked about some kind of museum here," Po said. They have their eyes on that old brick building across the street from Selma's store."

Po and Kate rounded the corner onto Elderberry Road, and Po pointed to a large, three-story building that used to house a hardware store before Home Depot moved into the mall on the edge of town. Today a For Sale sign was posted in one of the dirty windows.

Kate squinted to read the sign. "McKay Commercial Real Estate," she read. "Hah. Billy's everywhere."

"He's a go-getter, just like his father."

"Well, he charmed the socks off every teacher in Crestwood High," Kate said. "If he's half as good with his clients, he'll be very successful."

"And the voters. Eleanor told me yesterday that he may give the city a good deal on an old warehouse down near the river. They want to turn it into a halfway house."

"That doesn't surprise me. He actually did some good things at school, like chairing food drives. And though I don't mean to take away from his generosity, none of that will hurt his political career."

"No, you're right about that. He's planting seeds of goodwill. But if it helps the city in the process, more power to him."

Kate nodded. She had to admit Billy was doing a good job. She'd bumped into him several times since seeing the sign in the bookstore and had found him interesting, polite. Janna Hathaway was fortunate, and Kate suspected from the tight grip she kept on him that she was aware of that fact.

Kate and Po slowed down in front of the antiques store on the corner. A young couple from Kansas City had recently bought the old Windsor House Antiques after a scandal had sent the owner to jail. They'd done good things to it, the neighborhood association all agreed. A dark, elegant but sometimes foreboding space had taken on a bright look, with skylights and bright urns overflowing with flowers in every window. While it still held some priceless antiques, the store was more affordable now, and, although some old timers felt that elegant antiques deserved a more somber environment, Po considered the change a refreshing one.

Next door, Marla already had customers filling the front bay window of her bakery and café. The smell of cinnamon drifted out the open door, right along with Daisy Bruin, owner of the Elderberry Road florist shop.

"Morning ladies," she called out, her smile as wide as the huge muffin she held in her hand. "Life's good," she said with a grin and walked into her own shop.

Brew and Brie, Po's favorite shop for picking up Vermont white cheddar and a good Merlot, was closed up tighter than a drum. "Ambrose and Jesse are getting a late start, as usual."

"Big night. Those two are partiers."

They walked in front of Gus's bookstore just as he pulled up the blinds on the front window, readying himself for the Saturday crowd. Next to the store, a small open space held a few benches and gigantic flower pots, a favorite spot to read books from the bookstore while waiting for a table at the French Quarter—a plus for both owners. At this hour on a Saturday morning, it was deserted except for a collection of blue jays eating up last night's crumbs.

Po peered through the slated blinds on Jacques's windows but inside all was black. "That's strange. It's one thing for Ambrose and Jesse to sleep in, but Jacques is always here at this hour."

"Maybe he had a late night too. Maybe he and Laurel were out dancing." The thought was a hopeful one to both of them.

But Po rejected it. "It wouldn't matter. He's here every Saturday morning. Always. Selma will back me up." She began walking around the side, through the narrow patio to the back door.

Kate followed her. "Po, give the man some space. Everyone deserves a Saturday sleep in, even restaurant owners."

Po ignored her and tried the back door but it was locked. She stood tall and looked through the high window in the door. The delivery area and kitchen beyond were dark.

Po stood still, looking up and down the alley that ran behind the shops, then walked back toward the street, Kate hurrying to catch up. She looked at the front door with a confused look, then at Kate. "Kate, I realize I'm acting slightly erratic, but something is wrong. I can feel it."

"I'm late all the time and you never worry. I'm sure Jacques will be here in no time and you'll feel foolish for guarding his front door. Let's go." She tugged on the sleeve of Po's jeans jacket.

Reluctantly Po began to walk toward Selma's. But she couldn't shake the feeling that she was needed somewhere, and it wasn't at the big quilting table in the back of Selma's fabric store.

Kate locked her bike to the rack in front of the Parker Dry Goods Store and was relieved to see a smile begin to soften the angles of Po's face.

But before the smile reached a full curve, the door to the fabric shop swung open and Selma Parker walked outside, her face as chalky white as the sidewalk.

And Po knew without a smidgen of a doubt that she was right. Something was wrong.

"Jacques?" Po asked. Her heart squeezed tightly inside the wall of her chest.

Selma shook her head no, then yes. And then she grabbed them each by the arm and drew a confused Po and Kate back into the empty shop.

"Laurel," she said in the softest voice Po had ever heard Selma use. "Laurel St. Pierre is dead."

Chapter 6

By the time the remaining quilters arrived at Selma's, Kate, with urging from Po, had called P.J. Flanigan on her cell. He quickly confirmed the story already spreading across the small town as people turned on their radios and televisions and checked their phones and computers for the early morning news. The first reports were about a drowning in the river, relating it to a similar incident in which a college student had fallen off the bridge after a wild party several years before. But that story was soon replaced by a more sinister report.

"She was murdered," Kate said, returning to the table with her cell phone still in her hand. Her tone was of disbelief. "Laurel St. Pierre. We were just talking about her, maybe at the very moment she was being hurled into the river."

"Being hurled? What do you mean?"

Kate stared down at the phone as if to find the answer to Maggie's question.

"Like, who would do such a thing?" Phoebe's eyes filled her entire face, round and watery and caring, even though Laurel was a virtual stranger to her. "I'm bringing my babies up in this world? This is total craziness." She fingered one of several earrings curling up the edge of her ear.

"I can't imagine what poor Jacques is going through," Selma said. "He adored that woman. What a horrible time this is for him."

"We were with him, just last night," Susan said.

Selma nodded and explained to the others. "We had had a crazy day at the store and stopped in at the bistro, thinking a slight nip would help us sleep. Jacques came right over to the table."

"How was he?" Po asked.

"He looked tired, just like me. The man works all the time. We're not getting younger you know."

"Was Laurel there?" Kate asked.

"No," Susan said. "And it was crowded, being Friday night, so we were surprised."

"Some young gal was at the hostess desk," Selma said. "She looked like she should have been at Hooters. Jacques said he had insisted Laurel take the night off because she'd been working too hard. He had seen weariness in her eyes, he said."

"Who found her?" Maggie asked. She looked toward Kate. "The news report I heard on the way over was a little sketchy."

Kate drained her coffee mug. P.J. was discreet and she knew he wouldn't tell her more than what would soon be public knowledge. But his account was more complete than the news dribbles. "A couple of college. They were camping near that old quarry where the river starts to bend. P.J. said a large mound of boulders in the river's bend stopped her body from heading toward the Gulf of Mexico. At first they thought she drowned—but there was evidence of a blow to her head. They think now that that was what killed her. They don't know where she entered the river, but they know where she ended up."

"Oh, gross. I need more coffee." Phoebe jumped up and walked over to the sideboard, bringing the carafe back to the table. Her platinum mop of hair, no longer than a finger, framed a pixie face that lacked its usual wide grin. Even her glittery *I Love My Twins* T-shirt lacked luster.

At this time on a normal Saturday morning, the table would be filled with a dozen pieces of fabric, the sewing machine whirring, and laughter and talk would be spiraling up to the skylight that Selma had installed. Today the weight in the room was not from a stack of fat quarters, but from sadness and concern.

"I liked her," Leah said. She pulled a tissue from the pocket of her long jeans skirt and cleaned her rimless glasses, her eyes looking larger and sadder than usual. "She took a women's history class from me last semester. There was something intriguing about her, and I guess because we both came here from the East Coast, we had an odd bond. East Coast meets the Wizard of Oz, she said to me once, and we laughed over it. Sometimes she stayed after class and we'd talk. She seemed to want to learn things about Crestwood."

"What kind of things?" Po asked.

Leah brushed a thick strand of brown hair behind her ear. "Things like what was it like to live here? Who did I know here? Would I eventually leave? Odd questions."

"She didn't talk much to me," Kate said. "I tried a couple times, but she wasn't interested."

"But she watched you," Maggie said. "I'd catch her looking at you in the French Quarter sometimes. It was kind of weird."

"That's strange, Mags. I felt that, too—I was just telling Po about it. I asked her once if we had met before, even though I was pretty sure we hadn't. But she was abrupt and dismissive. Somehow I felt I had insulted her."

"Oh, pooh on that, Kate," Selma said. "You're a good-looking gal. People look at you." She took a drink of coffee, then frowned, as if doubting her own comment.

"Okay, so Kate's *not* attractive?" Maggie asked, looking at the shop owner.

Selma's smile was slight. "I'm thinking of Laurel looking at people. Scrutinizing them. Kate may have something there. Laurel watched people coming into the French Quarter diligently. Max Elliott and I talked about it once when we were sitting at the bar. Every time the door opened, Laurel was there, checking the customer out."

"So you were watching her. She was watching customers. We all people watch, don't we?" Po said.

"Well, sometimes it bordered on rudeness. Her scrutiny, not ours. It was almost like she was a bouncer in a bar, ready to confront someone or to throw someone out."

"Maybe she thought it was a part of her job. You know, to try and remember people's faces and names. People like that in restaurants. Laurel was a huge help to Jacques in getting the restaurant up and going. She might have wanted to recognize people better," Po said.

They all thought about that for a minute, until Maggie said. "Well, it's not important now, I guess. We'll never know why. It's Jacques we need to be thinking about."

"I agree," Leah said. "I worry about him. This is such a horrible thing. And he has no family here."

"They're all in France," Selma said. "And he works so dagnabbit hard he probably doesn't have any friends. I don't think he and Laurel really socialized."

"What about Laurel's family?" Kate asked.

"She never mentioned anyone to me," Susan said. "I think she grew up near New York."

"I drove by Jacques's house on the way over here," Phoebe said. "There were police cars in the driveway—but no sign of any others. Like normal cars that might belong to friends."

"Well, I consider him a friend. I think we all do. In the next couple days we at least can take some food over in case there are visitors," Po said. "Or in case he wants to talk. When Scott died, people saved me simply by being there, and that includes all of you."

"I can do that part, we all can. We talk a lot but we listen too. Cooking for Jacques, though, is a little like singing for Pavarotti," Eleanor said. "I shall certainly take over a fine bottle of French wine. I know he will like that. Therapeutic, anyway"

Selma sighed, her eyes focusing on piles of colorful fabric. "Maybe we all need a little therapy today. Working on Jacques's quilt might be just what we need. There's not much else we can do right now."

The group nodded, and as if some unseen stage director had given a cue, soft cloth bags appeared from beneath the table, the sewing machine hummed to life, and Leah filled the table with brightly colored swatches of fabric.

"Here's what we're doing," she said. "Susan and I have worked it all out. This is not going to be one of our democratic, do-whatever-moves-your-spirit kind of projects." She looked at them sternly over the top of her glasses. "Capiche?"

That brought nods and a slight lightening of the mood. No one ever questioned Leah's decisions when it came to design. Nor Susan's. The group felt nothing but gratitude to the two talented artists. As Kate often said, they made even her puny contributions look good.

"Good," Leah said, smiling.

Maggie raised her hand, a soulful look on her face. "Now don't forget."

"We haven't. You'll be doing sashes and borders, Maggie. Or one of the blocks. Not a bit of appliqué," Susan assured her. "I promise."

"Ah, there is a God," Maggie said.

"Just when I finally get my lines straight, you do this to us," Eleanor said, looking down at the intricate pattern. "I don't think there's a straight line in the whole darn quilt."

Susan had used graph paper and colored pencils to sketch the quilt for them to see. In the center, on the bottom half of the quilt, was a large pot, composed of different shapes of black and gray and silver fabric, pieced together in six small blocks. Above the pot were four large appliquéd fish, their bodies an intricate blend of wavy lines, with small yellow and black circles for eyes. Striped fins were flattened against the scaled bodies. Even when depicted in a simple, rough sketch, they could see the beauty and intricacy in the design, clear enough to elicit "ahs" and "oohs" from the quilters.

"Susan and I will design and make the fish, and they'll be appliquéd on the pieced background."

"This will be absolutely gorgeous," Po said.

"It's beautiful," Kate said. "I don't know if I can do this justice."

"You're getting better, Kate," Susan said. "Don't underrate yourself. Your photos inspired those fish."

The mood lightened slightly as the group leaned over the table, studying Susan and Leah's design. Graceful lines of steam curled up from the pot, and the pieced background, composed of blocks of deep gold, daffodil yellow, and soft tan, held the design in place. Tiny flecks of green and gold, which would be appliquéd on in the final stages, represented the bits of herbs and spices that made Jacques's bouillabaisse unique.

"I can almost smell that amazing soup," Phoebe said.

"Bouillabaisse, Phoebe," Kate said, "Boo-ya-baise." Her feigned French accent, imitating Jacques, brought smiles.

"Jacques will be so pleased." Po said softly.

"But only if we actually make it," Leah reminded them, determined not to let the sadness of the day overwhelm them. "So let's get to work. We've already cut up the pieces and made you each your own block patterns. I know Eleanor will only do her piecing by hand but you can decide for yourself. To work!"

Chapter 7

For more years than they cared to remember, Po and Leah Sarandon had met for breakfast at Marla's Bakery on Sunday mornings, a habit born of their husbands' love for early-morning golf. While the two men enjoyed fresh breezes walking the greens just east of town, their wives chose instead to settle at a small table near the front window of Marla's Bakery. Their twelve year age difference dissolved instantly in the heat of their shared passion for quilting and books and world issues.

Today the hum in the heated bakery was louder than normal. Leah looked over as a Marla approached their table. In addition to her baking skills, the baker never failed to season Po and Leah's breakfast with a generous dose of gossip.

The bakery proprietor moved to the side of their table like a cat with a whole nest of mice at the ready.

"Ladies," she said in an excited stage whisper, "have I got news for you."

Leah smiled at the familiar greeting, and Po suggested that maybe they needed coffee first. Preparation for whatever was to come out of Marla's wide mouth.

Marla filled their mugs, then pointed at a waitress to take an order from the next table, her eyes moving over the tops of heads, checking for empty plates or customers looking for checks. The room was nearly filled, and soon there would be a line out the door, with customers waiting on outdoor benches reading the Sunday paper.

"It's sad news about Laurel St. Pierre," Leah said in a kind voice, hoping to nip Marla's news in the bud.

"Awful," Marla said. She set the coffee pot down on their table and pressed her palms flat down beside it. "I know a young woman dying like that is horrible and all, sure it is, but Jacques may be better off without her."

"Marla, what an awful thing to say," Po said. "Jacques was crazy about Laurel."

"Doesn't mean she was good for him, Po. She could be nasty as all get out if she didn't like you. Ask Max Elliott—she couldn't stand that sweet man—I saw with my own eyes how she'd be rude to him. But that's not the worst of it."

Po poured a stream of cream into her coffee, then passed the pitcher over to Leah, and they both settled sat in their chairs, realizing they'd lost their effort to stay the conversation. Marla would have her stay.

"Rumor has it that Mrs. St. Pierre had gentlemen friends who were most definitely not of the French persuasion." Marla leaned over the table and looked back and forth between the two women. "Daisy Bruin saw that woman talking to a man in the alley, very cozy like, not two weeks ago. It wasn't Jacques or Jesse or anyone we know from the shops. And believe you me, they weren't talking about the weather."

"Daisy should keep her gossip to herself," Po said. "Good grief. What does talking to a man in an alley mean anyway? I've talked to men back there myself, Marla, and you never linked me romantically with anyone." Po's words were far more forceful than she felt. Thoughts of the recent encounter that Kate had witnessed at Riverside Park had interrupted her dreams all night long. But she continued anyway, her tone of voice uncharacteristically tight. "We need to support Jacques and help him through the funeral, not make burying his wife more difficult for him than it already is."

"Oh, phooey on you, Po, you sound like an old maid schoolteacher. Besides, there won't be a funeral." Her chin lifted up in a smug way, her head still, eyes on Po.

Po and Leah both looked at her. Po's brows lifted. "Okay, Marla, what do you know?"

"Heard it from Shelby Harrison. He comes in for a sack of cinnamon rolls every single Sunday morning before going over to his funeral home. Bill McKay and Max Elliott were in here talking business things. They do a lot of that lately. Anyhow, it seems Max handles Jacques's legal things just like he does everyone else's in town. So when Shelby spotted him, he walked over and in that hushed sort of voice he uses for business, he told him that when the police released the body, he was going to quietly take care of things for Jacques at his funeral home. Quick cremation. No funeral. Exactly like Jacques wanted."

Po sat back in the chair, pushing back her surprise. "Well, that's how it will be then. Whatever is best for Jacques. People need to do what's best for them."

"Or maybe what that young wife of his wanted," Marla suggested.

Po nodded, though she suspected Laurel hadn't given one thought to her own funeral arrangement. She was years too young to spend time thinking of urns or ceremonies.

"So the cremation surprises you?" Marla said, not wanting to let the topic drop. "Maybe it's a French thing."

Cremation didn't bother her at all, and from the look on Leah's face, she could tell her friend was in agreement—and worried about the same thing. Would Jacques be able to find the closure he needed without any kind of memorial? And what about family and friends? She hoped for Jacques's sake it was the right decision.

Not getting the kind of response she was looking for, Marla straightened up and scanned the small café, checking for customers needing coffee or checks, then picked up the pot she'd set on the table. "Well, ladies, stay tuned. There's more to this story than meets the eye. Trust my words." She spotted the Reverend Gottrey on the other side of the restaurant. He held one finger in the air, summoning service, and Marla hurried off, her wide backside weaving back and forth among the tables without toppling a single glass of water.

A young waitress appeared minutes later, a tray balanced in one hand. "Marla says you need comfort food," she said, and set down two plates heaped high with blueberry pancakes and small jugs of Vermont maple syrup off to the side.

Leah smiled up at her. "Marla is absolutely right." She shook out her napkin and slathered the top pancake with butter, then poured a thick stream of maple syrup across the top.

"It's far too early for Michigan blueberries," Po observed, reaching for the butter.

"She goes up every July, picks 'em fresh, then freezes 'em," the waitress explained.

Kate and Po dug in, concentrating on the plump juicy blueberries that filled the pancakes. But the emotion connecting the two friends across the blue-checkered tablecloth was not of food or Michigan blueberries.

Their thoughts were blocks away, thoughts of a friend alone with his grief. And a beautiful young woman robbed of life far too early.

* * * *

Po sat at her kitchen table several hours later, staring at the scraps of material that would magically come together to resemble a cooking pot.

She had taken the long way home, driving through Jacques's neighborhood. She slowed down when she reached his home. The front yard was perfectly kept, the house dark. Po drove on. When Scott died she had wrapped herself in writing and quilting, filling her calendar with events. She imagined Jacques in the kitchen of the French Quarter, mixing a creamy batch of crepes. Comfort in what he knew and loved.

But she'd brought the dark home with her and even when she settled down in the airy kitchen and family room—the hub of her life—she felt the gloom of a friend's tragedy.

From the fireplace end of the room, Po's ten-year-old golden retriever lifted his head from a slipcovered couch and looked as her. Po smiled, finding an odd wave of comfort in Hoover's eyes. Compassionate eyes. Something they'd be needing a lot of in the coming days.

But for right now, for the few hours she had left before the sun set, she would set compassion aside and think instead of the work of art they were piecing together for a bare wall in a friend's restaurant. Something constructive and soothing. The quilters had each taken pieces of Jacques's quilt home to work on. And among the twenty things on her to-do list, it was the most appropriate task for the day, since thoughts of Jacques were not far beneath the surface anyway.

Leah and Susan had outdone themselves on selecting the fabric. Po fingered a piece of cotton. The designers decided the quilt needed to fit into the casual bistro look of Jacques's restaurant, but they also wanted it to add color to the rough pale wall on which it would hang. They knew that a quilt in a restaurant would get abuse from odors and light and the air, but Jacques wanted it there anyway. Maybe they'd find an acrylic frame to protect it.

Po looked at the slender piece of cotton in her hand. The pattern was slight, a wavy line that added more texture than pattern to the piece. Six pieced blocks would form the round image of the pot, the sides glistening with sweat from the broth inside. Leah and Susan were geniuses in picking fabrics that created texture and feeling. The nubby blacks and grays and shiny silver patterns added interest, depth, and dimension to her pot. Amazing, she thought. Amazing women.

But the usual joy she felt in creating art out of small pieces of fabric was hard to find today. Within an hour, Po had put all her supplies back into the closet and had pulled a frozen blackberry breakfast loaf out of her freezer, placing it in a basket with muffins and jars of jam. Although she told herself she would give Jacques a few days with family before stopping by to pay her respects, her resolve was lost in the need to give the small round man a hug and a homemade pastry. She ran a brush through her hair and in minutes was driving the short distance to his house with hopes that he'd be there.

As she rounded the corner several blocks from Jacques's house, a tall, familiar figure, streaked auburn hair tossed to the wind, caught Po's eye. She pulled over to the curb and rolled down the passenger-side window, leaning across the seat. "So, Kate, you couldn't wait either?"

Kate ran over and rested her arms on the window frame. "If you don't mind my slightly sweaty body, I'll ride the rest of the way. Couldn't sleep much last night." She opened the door without waiting for a response and slid onto the front seat. "Can't get that little Frenchman off my mind. You can't either, it looks like. I thought maybe, well just seeing him, a quick hug, would be a good thing."

Po nodded as Kate strapped herself in. "I wanted to wait until relatives or whomever Jacques would surround himself with at a time like this were gone. But decided waiting wasn't going to help anyone. Myself included." She drove a few more blocks, then turned onto Jacques's street. Branches of aged oak and maple trees, already heavy with spring growth, hung over the street. Away from the road, up winding front walkways and brick driveways, tended flowerbeds of marigolds and daffodils spoke to easy peaceful lives, masking the sadness behind one neighborhood door.

Po pulled to the curb in front of the stately Tudor home. It was as still as it had been earlier in the day. And dark. But this time she noticed something she hadn't seen earlier.

Kate saw it too.

At the far side of the garage, partially hidden by several spirea bushes, was a car.

Laurel's car. They both recognized it immediately. There were few in Crestwood who had not seen the red Corvette one time or another, flying through town. Laurel drove fast, and usually with the top down, even in chilly weather. The sleek car and her long red hair blowing wildly in the wind were a familiar sight.

For one moment Po considered that it had all been a mistake. Laurel was home, probably getting ready for the evening shift at the French Quarter. Jacques was already at work, filleting fish and stirring a rich wine sauce. The two women sat in silence for a long moment, looking at the car as reality slowly settled in around them.

"It doesn't look like anyone's here," Kate said.

Po sighed and turned off the ignition. "Probably. But Jacques's car might be in the garage. If not, we can leave the breakfast basket at the door. Jacques probably doesn't need any of it, but it made me feel better."

Po lifted the basket from the back seat and they walked up the sidewalk toward the front door. As Kate lifted the brass knocker, the door suddenly opened.

Dwarfed by the doorframe stood a bedraggled, unshaven Jacques, his arms reaching out.

Without a word he pulled both women into a hug, his short arms stretching around them. Finally, he stepped away, motioning them into the house, and through the darkened foyer into an even darker living room.

Po glanced around at the long heavy drapes, covering every window in the room. She focused back on her friend. "We've all been concerned, Jacques. But we didn't want to intrude—"

Jacques shook his head to stop her words. "I am so glad you are here. Please, sit with me." He motioned toward a pair of brocade loveseats flanking a massive fireplace.

"First we need some light." Po walked over to the wall of mullioned windows and pulled on the cord, drawing open the drapes. Soothing streams of late afternoon sunlight streamed into the room. "There, that's much better. Sunshine helps the soul heal. We all need that."

Jacques sat opposite the two windows, leaning forward with his forearms resting on his knees. He wore an old pair of sweat pants that looked like they hadn't been taken off for a day or two. The rumpled figure seemed out of place in the expensively decorated room. A forlorn and lonely man, far older than his fifty years.

"What has happened to my life?" he asked them simply. His brown eyes were nearly black today, wet with sadness.

"This is as bad as it can be, Jacques," Po said. "But you have friends in this town. We are all here, and we will help you through this."

"Has Laurel's family arrived?" Kate asked. "Can we do anything for them? For you?"

Jacques shook his head. "There's no one. No family."

"Laurel had no family?"

"Oui," Jacques said as he rose from the couch. "She was a lonely, lost soul when I met her. An orphan."

"Well, she blossomed under your love," Po said, hiding her surprise.

"Laurel was a beautiful woman," Kate said, feeling the emptiness of her words before she spoke them. But the comment caused Jacques to lift his head and try to meet it with a smile.

"That was so important to her. To be beautiful. She had no money when we met. Barely two bills. She was a frail, drab waitress working two shifts in a diner I would never have gone into—except I spotted her through the window. The red hair, that's what I spotted. And there was something about her. A soul inside the tired body perhaps. So I went in and sat in a booth, and I smiled at her. She didn't smile at first, but I came back, lured her to my table with large tips. And finally a smile appeared.

"Soon she quit that awful place and I made sure she had whatever she wanted to let that beautiful soul flourish—spas and hair treatments and clothes and a life that allowed her to shine. I didn't even want her to work in my restaurant—but once we moved here and the house was settled, she insisted on coming in. She needed to get used to the town and meet the people, she said."

Kate listened carefully, looking now and then at the enormous painting of Laurel above the fireplace. Drab was a word that could never, even in her imagination, be applied to Laurel St. Pierre. "Was it hard for Laurel to move to Kansas from New York?"

Jacques shook his head vehemently. "No, no. It was hard for me!" He punched a fist into his chest and forced out a small laugh. "I loved New York, I loved my restaurant. I loved the commotion and the people, and I made fistfuls of money, more than in my dreams. But when Laurel came into my life, she wanted a quiet life—she was brought up in a small town. So, we found this little place, this empty storefront in this sweet little town. And we've been happy here, mostly—" His voice dropped off and he stood up, his fingers grasping the fireplace mantel as if for support. He closed his eyes and shook his round head slowly. "No, no," he murmured.

Po got and walked over to him. She said, "Don't pull away from those who care about you, Jacques. Please know we're here."

"That's music to my ears, Po. The police, they ask so many questions. They wonder if Laurel had enemies. Laurel, with enemies? How foolish and silly. There was no one who would hurt her. No one. She was a beautiful flower."

"Do you have any idea what happened, Jacques?"

"*Certainment*," he said. The French word shot through the air like a bullet, and for the first time that day the familiar spirit of the robust little Frenchman filled the room.

"Yes?" Po prompted.

"I know exactly what happened. It was a vicious robbery. Laurel always wanted much dollar bills in her purse. She then felt secure. So someone robbed her of her money and then the monster killed her so she wouldn't tell."

The words were said with the unflagging assurance that this was, indeed, the only possible scenario. The irrefutable truth.

"And the police, this is what they say?" Kate asked.

"They look for problems, they ask about boyfriends—what an awful thing to ask. Can you believe that? They ask about trouble in our marriage. Trouble? I would have died for my Laurel. I would have given my life for her."

Po and Kate looked at one another. The thought of P.J.'s news that Laurel St. Pierre had filed a complaint against her husband passed between them so loudly they were sure Jacques would hear it.

Then, looking back into Jacques's sorrowful eyes, Po heard something else—a conviction equally as loud: Jacques St. Pierre loved his wife without question. And whatever happened that night could not begin to touch the love she saw there.

"I know you loved her, Jacques," Po said softly. "I can't imagine what this must be like for you. But please know you have friends minutes away. We'll leave you now—I know you have many things to take care of—but we will be at your side. Know that." Po touched his arm and saw the effect of her words in his watery eyes.

Jacques switched on a light as they entered the darkened foyer. Directly ahead was a foyer table, but it was what was above the table that caught Kate and Po's attention. They stopped walking and looked again.

Hanging in front of them on the ten-foot wall was a beautiful quilt—a collection of brilliant blues and greens and yellows, swirling against a deep purple background. In the center of the swirls, emerging from the folds of the cloth, was a spectacular bird, so rich and textured they had to hold themselves back from reaching up to touch it.

Instead of words, they let out soft sounds of surprise and amazement and appreciation. A collective awe.

Jacques stood beside them, watching their pleasure.

"Where did you get this, Jacques?" Po asked. "It's amazing."

"It was Laurel's." Jacques bowed his head.

"Laurel made this?" Kate asked, not quite believing that could be the case.

He shook his head no. "It was a gift, she said. She cherished it. Sometimes, she'd take it down and lay it across the bed, fingering it, like child does a cherished blanket. I'd often find her there, the quilt across her knees. She touched it as if it were the most valuable thing in her life. I'd find her fixing small threads that came loose, sewing the edges. She cared for it as gently as the child we could never have."

A hushed silence followed Jacques's words as all three of them stood in a line, looking up at the quilt, as if standing in a museum before a featured exhibit.

"I suggested to her once that we put it in the restaurant, but she was very distressed at the thought. She would not consider it. It could only be here, in our home, in this place of honor. And she was the only person who could touch it, she told me."

Po looked at the quilt again, her eyes soaking in the fine detail, the lovely, perfect curves of the wings, the blend of appliqué and piecing. It was similar to what they were creating for Jacques's restaurant. She looked at the vines that wrapped around all sides of the quilt, twirling and curling like dancing nymphs.

"I am so pleased you like it," Jacques said, watching their eyes devour the quilt. "You ladies know so much about quilts. I said once we should invite you all over to see it, but no…" Jacques's sentence dropped off, and then he looked at them and said, almost apologetically, "She said this was private. Not for other eyes."

Po watched him look up again at the quilt. It was almost as if he were seeing images of Laurel in this piece of art that she had loved.

Jacques turned away, as if a light had burned his eyes. He walked to the door, holding it open for his guests and forced a smile to his lips. "Thank you, dear friend. Your visit to me today means very much."

Po looked back at the quilt, committing it to memory. Then she accepted Jacques's kiss to each cheek and followed Kate through the front door and to the car.

Kate climbed in and buckled her seatbelt, her eyes on Po as she sat unmoving behind the steering wheel. She was staring straight ahead, with a faraway look as if seeing things not quite in focus. "What's the matter? You look like you've seen a ghost."

Po glanced back at Jacques's house, then strapped her own seatbelt in place and looked at Kate. "I don't know, Kate. Maybe I have. It's that quilt. I would swear on a stack of Bibles that I've seen it before, and it wasn't hanging on Jacques's wall."

Chapter 8

The need to buy groceries and clean the family room before friends arrived for supper kept Po from dwelling on the seemingly familiar quilt, though images of the bird were in her mind's eye as she prepared the béarnaise sauce for tonight's fillets and stacked buffet dishes on the end of the table for dinner. She revisited the images, the colors, committing them to memory to return to later. When P.J. and Kate arrived a short while later, Po sent them out back to manage the grill while she went upstairs to take a quick shower and try to wash away the disturbing thoughts.

"You two are in charge," she had said. "Make sure everything is wonderful."

P.J. feigned a bow. "You've any doubts, madame?" He held the door open for Kate and followed her through the porch and outside to the grill while Po retreated upstairs.

"Something is wrong with Po," P.J. said, balancing the tray of meat in one hand and the salt and pepper in the other. He looked back up to the porch.

"She's worried about Jacques." Kate set the grilling tools on a small table beside a bowl of mushrooms. She breathed in a lungful of brisk evening air and looked away, to the back of the yard and a thick border of maple and oak and cherry trees. A kids' haven. It was there that the Paltrow kids and their cousin Kate—as everyone called her, even though they all knew she wasn't really related—played hide and seek and built tree houses and forts and ate Robinson Crusoe sandwiches that Po made for them—buns thick with ground ham and cheese and a special sauce. It was their getaway, a private place. She suddenly longed for all that it reminded her of: carefree days and laughter and nothing more serious than skinned knees to worry about.

P.J. opened the heavy cast-iron lid and poked the coals to life. Crimson embers lit up the air. He turned to Kate, his face serious. "Much as I hate to say this, Po may have something to worry about."

Kate abandoned her memories and looked back at the grill. She handed P.J. a long fork. "What is that supposed to mean?"

P.J. speared each thick steak and placed it on the grill. "All I mean is that this whole thing doesn't look good for Jacques right now."

"P.J., you're crazy," Kate said. Her fingers curled into fists at her side as if to keep her from shoving P.J.'s words back into his mouth.

"Hey, calm down, Kate." He brushed the top of each steak with a thin layer of butter and olive oil. For a moment the sizzle of fat dripping on the coals was the only noise in Po's backyard. P.J. concentrated on the grill, his eyes not meeting Kate's.

When Kate spoke again, her voice was softer, but still edged with anger. She knew it didn't make sense. And she wasn't blaming P.J., not really. But he was the messenger. And the news wasn't good. "It's just that Jacques is such a kind, good man," she said. "And if you could have heard him earlier today, you'd never in a million years doubt his love for his wife. And what about the guy I saw in the park with Laurel? And the rumor mill carries other meetings she's had with guys. Laurel was beautiful. I mean…I mean it seems there are other people the police should be looking at, right?"

"Right. And all of that is being investigated, Kate. I don't mean anyone is ready to arrest Jacques. But there's so much hearsay spinning around, and it takes time to separate rumor from fact. Your description of the man you saw her with includes half the county. And it's the same with the other tips coming in. Mostly without names. Oh, except for that little waiter at the restaurant everyone thought was in love with her. But Jacques is the one she was calling abusive. He's the one on the police report."

"But he loved her more than you can imagine, P.J. I'm sure of that." Kate heard her own hollow words, flimsy words.

"I'm not doubting the man's love. But people sometimes do bad things, even to people they love. Take you—" He tried to joke her out of the moment. "Look how nasty you're being to me—and God knows you're crazy about me."

But Kate would have none of it. "This is one of the things that's desperately wrong with our legal system. We say people are innocent until proven guilty, but then the news gets out there, and the whole world treats you like you're guilty without any proof whatsoever."

The news that Laurel had called the police on Jacques had somehow leaked out, startling nearly anyone who knew Jacques and had ever felt his gracious hospitality in the French Quarter bistro. "A small-town restaurateur may have some connection to his wife's murder," the reporter on the Kansas City, Missouri, news channel had announced, and then went on to talk of possible marital discord that an unidentified source had passed the reporter's way.

"I don't know how that story ever got on the news tonight. I guess it's the weekend doldrums—there's nothing else to talk about. But it was all some reporter's conjectures, or some neighbor reporting having seen her out on the steps that night, and then building a story around the police appearance. The police wouldn't say anything like that at this point, even though it was pretty true."

Kate handed P.J. a cup of wine sauce for the meat. "So, the police... well, a lot of you know Jacques. I see uniforms in the French Quarter all the time. So you all must know Jacques is innocent?"

"The police aren't convinced you're innocent, Kate. The guys assigned to the case are just beginning to look into it. Everyone has to be looked at. The guy in the park—whoever he is— the people in the restaurant. Friends of Laurel's. It was a murder, Kate."

"Are you two almost ready with the steaks?" Po called through the screen door. She felt like a new woman, refreshed, her tan slacks and bright blue sweater masking the afternoon's emotion.

"Five minutes max, boss lady," P.J. called back. He turned a row of large white mushrooms on the top burner and brushed them generously with garlic butter.

P.J. had become Po's barbecue doyen in recent months, a role that had once been Scott Paltrow's. For years Scott had welcomed friends and neighbors on quiet nights, an excuse to fire up his grill. The gatherings were sorely missed after Scott died. But when P.J. expressed interest in resurrecting the old heavy grill—Po had gladly accepted, much to friends and neighbors delight. Po saw it as another excuse of P.J.'s to hang out with Kate, who seemed to spend at least one meal a weekend at her home.

But whatever the reason P.J. came, his barbecue skills nearly as fine as her husband's had been, and Po took full advantage of it.

Tonight was no exception, but she sensed a private discussion going on between him and Kate and moved back into the kitchen, assuming he'd be attentive enough to keep the steaks from burning.

"Just for the record, P.J.," Kate said, once Po had gone back inside, "Jacques is a good man. We both know that. And I'm not so sure his wife was a perfect person. In fact, I suspect there were plenty of people who wouldn't be terribly sad to have Laurel St. Pierre off their radar screen. People you haven't even thought of yet."

"That's a little harsh, Kate."

Kate was silent. She had no basis for her strong words, but she felt them deep inside of her. Laurel had always made her uncomfortable, and instinct told her there were things about the woman that would surprise all of them, including Jacques.

P.J. watched the mix of emotion clouding Kate's face. "It'll be okay, Katie," he said. His voice was gentle now. "If there's something the police need to know about Laurel, we'll find it out. The truth will come out. Honest, it will. Now help me with these steaks. Po will have my head if they're all well done. Besides, we need to fatten you up." He piled the meat on the platter Kate held. Next he scooped the mushrooms into a bright blue ceramic bowl and tried to lighten the mood. "We make a great culinary team, Kathleen Anne Mary Simpson. Next stop, Top Chef. But for the moment let's go inside and accept the well-deserved praises of our hungry friends."

Kate looked at him for a minute, then shook her head and allowed the small smile he was waiting for. "You can be so absolutely irritating, Flanigan—always seeing all sides of everything. But you make it impossible to stay mad at you. I hate that." She turned and headed for the porch door. "Fatten me up, my foot," she muttered, and walked on inside.

Po looked at each of the steaks, then lightly pressed the fleshly part of her palm down on one of the fillets. She looked up and beamed at P.J. "It's perfect. Medium rare. The others can pick their own." She washed her hand in the sink and set the platter on the table.

"I think we'll be a small group tonight." She looked to the other end of the room where Phoebe was curled up on the couch with Jimmy and the twins. Jimmy was reading all of them a story about a little boy who gave a moose a muffin.

Gus Schuette and his wife, Rita, sat with Eleanor, debating the merits of dirty martinis. Po was glad Rita had come; her irreverent wit and outspoken opinions provided fodder for lively conversation. Wrapped up in her small Latin body was enough fuel to fly an airplane, her husband claimed.

"Max Elliott said he's coming by," Rita called out to Po. "I think he has the hots for you, Po."

They all laughed, Po along with them. The last thing she wanted in her life was a romantic entanglement. But she was happy that Max was coming—she hoped there'd be a chance to ask him subtly about Laurel St. Pierre. She was surprised at Marla's gossip—she hadn't known Max even knew Laurel. Besides, the thought of anyone not liking Max Elliott was difficult to imagine. She'd known the accountant for a long time and the only negative thing she'd ever heard about him was that he didn't like KU basketball. A Villanova fan, he boasted, proud of his Philadelphia roots.

As if on cue, a knock at the front door announced Max's presence. "I've brought a couple more friends," he called from the front door, then walked on in. "Knew you wouldn't mind."

Max was assisted by a short cane—the only sign of a serious car injury the year before. "Hey everyone, you all know Bill McKay, and his lovely fiancée, Janna." Max bowed toward the woman standing demurely beside the imposing Bill McKay.

"Of course we do. Welcome," Po said, wiping her hands on a dishtowel and hurrying across the room to greet the new arrivals. She wasn't used to greeting people, but somehow the two newcomers were different. The label "guests" fit them but not the others who had settled into the back family area of Po's home, acting as if it were their own.

"I'm happy you came," she went on. "Make yourself at home. Max, get them drinks, and if you don't know everyone, introduce yourself around."

Kate was standing near the kitchen table chewing on a cheese stick. "I can't imagine Billy not being recognized. There are more posters with his picture on it than on the entire post office wall."

Bill laughed along with the others and made the rounds of hellos. He picked up Phoebe's Emma and lifted her to his shoulders, caring the delighted toddler around the room.

Janna followed close behind him, greeting everyone graciously and quietly. She wore a blue silk jacket and slacks, perfectly tailored and slightly out of place with the casually dressed crowd. She was slightly ill at ease, Po thought, but that was understandable—she was the new person in a roomful of people who had lived in Crestwood nearly all their lives. "Janna, come meet the other best two-year-old in the room." She took Janna's hand and led her over to the couch, where Phoebe urged her to sit next to her. In minutes Phoebe had plopped one twin on her lap, along with the moose book, and suggested Janna finish it for Jude, who was cuddling up nicely to his new reader.

Janna went along with it, even tousling the little boy's hair and working hard to add voices to the book's characters. She had clearly been brought up right—gracious, polite, and she looked you in the eye when she spoke to you. But the smile had a difficult time staying in place, and beneath it, Po sensed that the young, well-bred woman had found out early that her family's wealth couldn't buy everything. Beneath her wealth, Janna Hathaway was plain looking and quiet, as if the recipe had been followed perfectly, all the ingredients in place, except for that unknown, indescribable one that made one person stand out and another fade into the background. Beside her, Phoebe, filled with that magic ingredient, sparkled liked a diamond.

At least Janna is in good hands, Po thought. Phoebe had a knack for collecting people and making them comfortable.

Across the room, Gus Schuette was patting Bill on the back, applauding his decision to run for mayor. "You can do it, Billy boy. Bring some new blood to this town."

"The town needs more than blood," Rita cut in. "What do you intend to do for Crestwood, Bill? Give me the facts, not political jibber jabber."

Bill laughed, but answered immediately. "Well, for starters, I love this town."

"Oh, phooey with that. Sure, sure, sure. Of course you do. We all do. But no matter what they say, love doesn't always make a town go around. What will you do other than cut ribbons?"

Bill ran his fingers through his hair, slightly taken back. "Got it. Okay. I'm looking into getting council support to fix up some old buildings for the town that my father doesn't know what to do with, using them for social service needs. Get a free health clinic on the ballot. Make sure the fire department gets the new equipment it needs. I guess that's really why I want to be mayor—so I can give back to this town that gave so much to my family."

Rita nodded. And finally she smiled. "Those are good things. But you may have to toughen up a little, Bill McKay, if you want to be a politician," Rita said. "I almost had you there for a minute."

Her husband came up beside her and wrapped an arm around his wife's narrow shoulders. "Stick around Rita and she'll do the toughening for you. It's that Latin blood."

Bill granted him that and smiled at his wife. "I have a lot to learn about politics here. But I have a feeling it might have room for the likes of me."

Po watched the lopsided smile, and decided that Bill McKay might be right. She walked over to the small group. "I remember your father saying you'd be a politician someday. He must be proud of this turn in your career."

"We're all proud of Bill," Janna said, looking up from her book. She smiled over at Bill. "Both sets of parents know Bill has nowhere to go but up."

Po watched affection color Janna's face but what was more pronounced was the determination in her words. Bill responded with a nod in her direction and a smile that Po couldn't quite read. He shrugged, offered a half-smile, and joked, "She has me in the White House in five years."

Max Elliott raised a wine glass. "Here, here, to Mayor McKay."
A noisy toast followed, along with well wishes for Bill's campaign and plans. "And now," Po said, "before we propel Billy directly into the White House, I suggest we eat. Pick up a plate from the sideboard before P.J.'s fine steak turns cold." Friendly laughter nudged the crowd around the table and in minutes plates were heaped full of hot rolls and sweet butter, mounds of basil and corn pasta, and P.J.'s juicy fillets and béarnaise sauce.

Po didn't have a chance to talk to Max Elliott alone until the meal was almost over and empty plates began to stack up on the dining room table. She was removing pies from the refrigerator when he appeared at her side.

"Need help, Po?" He set his wine glass on the counter and took the pies from her hands.

"Thanks, Max. Just set those on the counter."

Po took out a pie cutter and stack of dessert plates. "It was nice of you to bring Billy and Janna, Max. I don't think Janna knows many people."

"And doesn't make friends easily, as far as I can tell," he said. "I was meeting with Bill about some company matters and knew you wouldn't mind if I invited them."

"Are you helping Bill with his political plans?" Po asked.

"Not so far. Though I'll help him if I can. But I did legal and financial work for the family's realty company years ago, and Bill has asked me to help him out with a few things to get the company back on track." Max picked up the knife and began slicing through layers of coffee ice cream, thick hot fudge, and a thin, crusty layer of crushed pralines. "Sinful, Po," he moaned, lifting a wide slice and sliding it onto a plate.

"But good for the spirit every once in a while," Po said. She placed a fork on each plate. "Max, I've been wanting to ask you about Jacques. Have you had a chance to speak with him?"

Max took a drink of his wine, then shook his head no.

Po saw the furrows on his brow deepen. He seemed to want to say something to her, but instead, he lifted his wine glass again and drained it.

"Max, what is it?"

Max picked up the tray of pie plates and looked at Po. "The truth is, I wanted to go over to Jacques's as soon as I heard the news. I like him very much. We've spent time together socially as well as my helping him with the books. But frankly, Po, I'm not the right person to be with him right now. Make of that what you will."

Before Po could question him further, he walked back to the family room area and a chorus of voices welcoming the ice cream pies. Po watched him as he handed out the plates of dessert, wondering what in the world could cause such uncharacteristic behavior in this gentle man she had come to respect and like very much. It wasn't like Max at all. And she wondered briefly how many other relationships would become awkward because of the murder of a young woman none of them really knew.

Chapter 9

Sunday night gatherings usually ended early so everyone could get home in time to prepare for another week. Tonight was no exception. Max was the first to go, and Po regretted saying anything to him about Jacques. He seemed troubled when he left, and after a quick kiss on the cheek and a thank you, was out the door without another word. The others followed soon after, although Eleanor lingered behind, helping Po put away the last of the dishes.

"Po, you've been distracted tonight. Out with it," Eleanor demanded, pouring the last of the coffee into her mug.

Po wondered if it was good for Eleanor to have all that caffeine so close to bedtime, but she stayed quiet, knowing Eleanor would do what she pleased, no matter what anyone said.

"It's Jacques isn't it?" Eleanor said abruptly. She eased herself into a kitchen chair, rubbing one hip. "It's awful that he's going through all this."

Po nodded. It was awful, and confusing, and it was affecting people she cared about. But she knew instinctively that whatever was bothering Max tonight was something she didn't have any right to talk about with others. But there was one thing that she needed to talk about. And Eleanor was the perfect person.

"Eleanor," she began, "something happened today that is plaguing me. I saw a quilt hanging on the wall of Jacques's home." The image of the beautiful bird had remained with Po all evening. She described it to Eleanor in detail, the artful swirl of the fabric pieces, the brilliant colors that made the bird stand out in bold relief. "But the thing that is bothering me, El, the thing that I can't shake, is the almost certain thought that I've seen it before."

"You probably did," Eleanor said, sitting down at Po's wide table, now empty of the platters it held earlier. "Many people make the same quilt, Po, you know that. And from your description, it sounds lovely. Other people have probably used the same pattern."

"It wasn't that kind of quilt, El. It was intricate, unique. I don't think the pattern would have been easily duplicated, and even if it had been, it was the kind of artwork that you wouldn't want to pass on to others. It was so personal. But for the life of me, I can't remember where I've seen it before."

"Maybe someone did an article on it. Or you saw it at a quilt show. Houston, perhaps? We've certainly been to plenty of shows, and it would explain how you'd seen one from the East Coast."

"That's a possibility." Po considered Eleanor's ideas as she poured herself a cup of tea. She sat down across from Eleanor. "Jacques wanted to invite all of us to the house to see the quilt, but Laurel refused. No one was to see it."

"Laurel wasn't the most sociable person in the world. She probably didn't want a bunch of us tramping through her personal space."

As always, Eleanor's practical reasoning made sense. But Po couldn't absorb it as easily as she sometimes did. "That might be true. But it's a shame. Things that beautiful should be shared. No matter. But I sure wish I could remember exactly where I've seen it before. It will plague me in an awful way."

"It will come to you when you stop thinking about it," Eleanor said philosophically. "Believe me, I'm the expert on memory lapses. And things usually float back. Or not." Tiny lines around her clear blue eyes moved outward as she laughed. "But I will stop by Jacques's house to pay my respects and see it for myself. Now you have me curious." She eased herself up from the chair.

"Good. Maybe between the two of us, we will have a whole memory."

"Or not," Eleanor said, and headed for the door, her cane tapping on the floor as she went.

Chapter 10

By Tuesday, Po's thoughts of the bird quilt were buried beneath a cloud of more ugly matters: rumors.

"They're so huge, they could choke a horse," Selma told Po as they scurried across the campus of Canterbury College. The college auditorium was just ahead, where Leah's evening lecture on women in the 1960s was about to begin. A brisk breeze caused the two women to hug their jackets tight to bodies and keep their steps lively. Selma shoved her hands into her pockets. "It seems everyone and her brother has a story to tell about Laurel St. Pierre."

"Kate stopped by this morning on her way to that photography class she's taking. She can barely speak to P.J., she said. She wants him to publicly declare Jacques innocent."

"Maybe he should," Selma said. "Ridiculous thought that such a sweet man would do such a thing."

"Of course it's ridiculous. But with all these rumors spreading, the police need to look at everything."

"That gossipy column in the online town bulletin suggested that there's a whole army of men who know Laurel, and not in the way any husband would approve."

"That same newsletter declared improprieties about Eleanor when she hosted a political dinner the columnist didn't approve of," Po reminded her, nodding toward Eleanor's three-story mansion on the corner of the campus.

Selma laughed. "I remember. Eleanor loved it."

"But you have a point, Selma. Even though the rumors may be nonsense, the fact is that there's a smidgen of truth mixed in. Laurel did place a domestic violence call just days before she was killed. And she was seen being cozy with at least one unnamed man, maybe more. And when there's a bit of truth involved, rumor and truth become mixed until you can't tell one from the other."

The truth was that Po was worried sick over Jacques and all the gossip spinning around him. And she knew that the phone call Laurel made to the police wasn't anything that made him look better. It indicated marital trouble, even though Jacques denied it. He had told Po earlier that day that he was going to reopen the restaurant, just to have something to do. Would people interpret it as a lack of grieving? Po thought she might talk to Jacques about it, just to let him know that appearances could matter in a small town like Crestwood. Maybe he didn't know that; maybe it was different in France. She knew why he wanted to work—she was the same. For some, grieving was best woven into a productive life to keep it from becoming suffocating and unbearable. But she would tell Jacques to go slow, to take time for himself, too.

Selma held open the door to the Canterbury College auditorium and the two women walked into the lobby. "Looks like a good crowd," Selma observed. Leah's lectures were popular, and in addition to students and faculty, townspeople often came as well.

"There's Janna Hathaway," Po said, noticing the young woman standing near the lobby windows.

Po caught her attention and waved her over. "I'm happy to see you here, Janna. We share an interest in women's history, I guess."

Janna smiled and explained that Bill had suggested it. He had a business meeting with Max and some others that evening. "He thought it'd be good for me to be aware of things going on in the college community."

Po was disappointed, hoping that Janna's motives were personal rather than political. But she quickly swallowed the unkind interpretation and introduced her to Selma. "Selma has the most amazing fabric in her store that you'll find anywhere."

Janna smiled and shook Selma's hand. "Bill and I will be having some things made for the wedding. I'll bring my mother's decorator by some day."

"When is the wedding?" Selma asked.

"Not for nearly a year. My mother said it will take that long to get everything prepared, though I'd prefer to run off and get married tomorrow."

"Why don't you?" Selma asked. "One of my daughters did that. I was briefly disappointed, I must admit, but she was shy and didn't want all the hoopla. She'd have had an upset stomach for a month if we'd insisted on it. We had a great picnic celebration a few weeks later and everyone was happy."

Janna didn't smile. "That's not the way it works in my family. One doesn't cross Charles Hathaway."

Janna said her father's name in the way one talked about a foreign dignitary—with distant respect and no warmth. Po felt a wave of pity for her. "Would you like to sit with us?" she said. "Kate may be along as well."

But it wasn't until the question-and-answer period that followed the intriguing lecture on women leaders during the '60s Civil Rights movement—that Kate slid into the seat next to Po. "Sorry," she whispered. "I got caught up in cropping some shots I took today. But there's some I especially want you to have so I brought them along. How about we go for coffee after?"

Janna excused herself right after the lecture, but Selma, Kate, and Po grabbed Leah and headed for the college coffee shop, gathering around a corner table. They curled their fingers around mugs of strong coffee and, after letting Leah know she was amazing and they had learned a lot, they looked at Kate.

"Okay. What's up?" Po asked.

Kate pulled a handful of photos out of a large tote bag and spread them across the tabletop. "I wanted you to see what I did today."

Po looked at the photos, shuffling them with one finger. Toward the edge of the collection her finger stopped moving. She picked up a large eight-by-ten photo and stared at it. Several others of the same subject were beneath it.

"It's the quilt. Where did you get this, Kate?"

"I went over to Jacques's and offered to take some shots of it because it's so beautiful. He was pleased, so I enlarged a couple." She looked at Selma and Leah. "Po is trying to remember where she's seen it before, and I thought having this might help her remember."

"It's incredibly beautiful," Leah said, holding one of the photos up to the light.

Selma slipped her glasses on and leaned toward Leah. "Oh my Lord," she exclaimed, grabbing the photo directly out of Leah's hands and staring at it in disbelief. She looked at Po.

"I know exactly where you've seen this quilt before, Po Paltrow. You've seen it in my shop—a whole lot of years ago. And I'll tell you this much—it wasn't made by Laurel St. Pierre."

Chapter 11

Po stared at Selma. Then she looked at the largest of the photos and examined it carefully, this time remembering it against the plain painted wall in Selma's shop. When she finally spoke, her eyes were wide in disbelief. "Esther Woods," she said softly.

"Exactly. I'd know that quilt anywhere. In fact, I talked Esther into letting me display it in the shop during an October quilt competition years ago. That's where you saw it, Po."

"Who? What are you talking about?" Kate asked.

"I'm in the dark, too," Leah said. "I never heard of Esther Woods."

"Esther lived in Crestwood before you moved here, Leah," Po said. She looked at Kate. "And you probably would never have met her. She lived north of your neighborhood, near the highway. But she kept to herself."

"Lived?" Leah asked.

"Esther died years ago," Po said.

"Of a broken heart, if you ask me," Selma said.

"But the actual cause was an auto accident. Her husband was driving—"

"Driving drunk, Po. He was drunk as a skunk," Selma said. She took her glasses off and set them on the table.

Po nodded and explained to Kate, "Al Woods was a nasty man."

"He drove Esther and himself directly off the bridge just west of town," Selma finished.

"That's a terrible story," Kate said. She picked up one of the photos and looked again at the beautiful bird caught up in the still-vivid colors of the pieced background design. "But I still don't understand how the quilt got on Jacques's wall—if, in fact, it's the same one. Jacques was clear that it belonged to Laurel."

Po shook her head. "I can't imagine how Laurel got her hands on it. Unless Eleanor was right and there are copies of this quilt. If Laurel's quilt was the original, maybe Esther had a copy of the pattern and made hers from that."

"No, absolutely not," Selma said. She drained her coffee cup and set it down on the table. Deep wrinkles creased her forehead. "That was Esther's pattern, Esther's quilt. The woman had little in her life that she was proud of. The bird quilt was one of those few things. She designed it, pieced and appliquéd it, and quilted every single stitch herself. I guarantee it."

"So maybe she passed the pattern on to others," Leah said.

Selma shook her head. "I can't be positive she didn't, but my heart tells me she'd never have given it away. I didn't know Esther well—no one did because Al Woods was so possessive that she rarely ventured out. She was a seamstress—worked her little fingers to the bone, so she sometimes came into the store for thread and other sewing supplies, but not often. But I did know her feelings for her bird quilt, as she called it. She was so proud of it, and when I asked her if I could display it, you'd have thought she'd won the lottery. I think the quilt represented that part of her that was good and whole and happy, and she would never have allowed others to copy it, at least not knowingly. I'd bet my life on it."

"Some people can look at a quilt and figure out the pattern—Susan does that sometimes," Leah said.

"That's true," Selma admitted.

"But look closely at this quilt," Po said, holding a close-up photo of the bird up to the light. "It's so intricate. It's all coming back now. I don't think it could be a copy. I remember the blue and green thread circling around the gold streaks in the bird's wings. And the tiny gold French knots at the tips of the wings."

"Do you suppose Jacques can shed some light on it?" Leah asked. She drained her cup and slipped her arms into the sleeves of her sweater.

"Maybe," Po said. "We didn't talk about it much the other day. Did he say anything to you, Kate?"

Kate shook her head. "I don't think he knew much more. He just knew that Laurel loved it, so he loved it too."

Leah moved the photos of the quilt around on the table like pieces of a puzzle, seeing it from different angles, admiring the fine design. One picture, slightly stuck beneath the others, came loose, and Leah picked it up. "What's this, Kate?"

Kate leaned over and looked at the photo. She quickly took it from Leah's hand. "Oh, I didn't mean to include that one." She bit down on her bottom lip and looked from Leah to Po, then Selma. "I didn't know I had this picture until I downloaded my camera photos onto the computer. I think Amber must have taken it. She's a talented gal in a class I sometimes sub in. I ran into her in the park and let her play with my camera for a while." She paused and stared hard at the photo, her brows pulling together. Her heart had nearly leapt out of her chest when she'd discovered the photo an hour before. It was a clear shot of Laurel St. Pierre in the arms of another man. She'd called P.J. immediately, but he didn't pick up. She had left a message, and then remembered a meeting he had so his cell was probably muted. "I printed it out to pass along to P.J. and he can do what he wants with it," she said.

"P.J.?" Leah looked more closely at the picture. She frowned. "Is that Laurel St. Pierre?"

"Yes," Kate said. "She was in the park that day—I think I mentioned it to you, or you, Po. I didn't know it was Laurel at first. They—Laurel and this man—were standing up that slight rise in the park, near a grove of trees, kind of hidden. When they stepped out of the shadow, I realized it was Laurel—and a man. But I wasn't aware that Amber had taken their picture—I wasn't paying that much attention."

"The police will want to see this right away, Kate," Po said.

"That's my plan."

"Oh, my," Selma said. "It's one thing to hear the rumors, but quite another to have a photo of it."

"I almost felt guilty watching them that day," Kate said. "I didn't intend to intrude. But then after Laurel was killed, I told P.J. what I'd seen, but without a description, they couldn't do much except include it in with all the other things people were saying about Laurel."

"But now you have a picture," Leah said. "This might be good, Kate."

"Maybe it will help Jacques," Po said.

"I hope so."

Selma put her glasses back on and looked carefully at the photo. "He looks vaguely familiar. But I can't place him." The picture was passed around and examined carefully.

"Maybe it's someone Laurel knew before they moved here, someone from back east," Leah offered.

"And maybe it's someone who might have a motive for killing her," Kate said.

"From the looks of that photo, that's not what's on his mind." Selma looked at it again, then put it back down on the table.

"Maybe," Kate said. "But at least it's someone else for the police to concentrate on." She scooped up the pictures and slipped them into an envelope. She stood and put on her jean jacket.

The others gathered their purses and coats and pulled out dollar bills to tuck beneath the napkin holder as a student waitress came by to collect their cups.

Kate looked down at the table as if she were still looking at the picture, focusing in on that moment in time. "When I suspected the woman was Laurel, I kept watching them for a minute, trying to bring her into focus, trying to be sure of who it really was, I guess. And that's when I saw something Amber's shot didn't capture. She caught the kiss, but there was more. Laurel—and whoever he is— pulled apart shortly after. They seemed to be talking for a minute, and then the whole lovely scene was shattered by an angry slap. And I think it was Laurel who was doing the slapping."

Chapter 12

Wednesdays were writing days for Po, but a restless night left her mind foggy. A run along the river would put her in a better frame of mind, she thought. Perhaps it would bring some writing inspiration and distance her a little from things she couldn't do anything about. It was worth a try, though she suspected it might take more than a run to get her back on track.

The morning was brisk, and the air energized Po as she moved along the meandering paths, her slick red pants making swishing noises as she ran slowly along the path. Riverfront Park was nearly empty this morning, the quiet and solitude providing the venue she needed to sift through her tangled thoughts.

Kate's pictures of the quilt had unleashed something inside her—a nagging, uncomfortable feeling. And she suspected it would get worse before it got better. She felt an irrational need to sort through this mess they were all mired in. Esther Woods's bird quilt weighed heavily on her mind. Such a lovely work of art, and sitting there in all its glory on Jacques's wall. But something wasn't right. Something about it ending up in that house. In Laurel St. Pierre's possession. It was like reading through a quilt pattern that suddenly included the wrong colors or a triangle and a square motif that couldn't possibly come together within the area indicated. Only Laurel could tell them, could make sense of it all. And Laurel certainly wasn't giving any answers.

The river was calm today as Po ran along its edge. It had been swift the night Laurel had died. She looked across the narrow waterway, where the path continued but the terrain was less developed, rugged and craggy with overgrown weeds and thorny bushes. She wondered where Laurel had met someone on that path—and why. The police hadn't said where

Laurel had been thrown into the river, only where her body had been found. But it didn't matter much, Po supposed. The path ran all the way past the bridge and for a couple of miles south, where a smaller bridge crossed the river and connected the walking path to the one Po ran on now. It could have been anywhere along the way and ended in the same grisly way. She shivered and rubbed her arms against the chill as the grim reality of Laurel's murder took hold. Then she headed up one of the small paths away from the riverbank and back toward the Elderberry Road neighborhood and her own home.

As she neared Elderberry Road, she slowed down, then turned in behind Selma's shop and began running down the deserted alley. The sight of Jacques's van behind the French Quarter gave a lift to her spirits—any sign of normalcy coming from the grieving Frenchman was a good thing. She ran close to the restaurant, happy to see the kitchen windows open wide and sounds of life coming through the screens. The smells floating through the windows turned into images—steamed mussels swimming in garlic butter, French onion soup with Jacques's home-baked croutons floating on the top. Now if only she could help dispel the ugly rumors that swirled about the chef's little round head, life would be much better, indeed.

Po slowed to a stop behind the restaurant and stretched one leg, leaning into it, her eyes lifted to the back of the restaurant and the high kitchen windows on its west corner. Maybe this would be a good time to coax Jacques into talking about the bird quilt. A glass of water would be welcome, too. And a good excuse.

As Po brought her body upright, she spotted Jacques's blunt profile just inside the open kitchen window, but before she could head for the door, he turned away from the window and his voice rose in startling anger. "Vicious man! Judas!" he called out. "You were my friend and you betrayed me!"

Another voice, unfamiliar, muttered an answer. The man's voice was distant and Po imagined him standing near the door to the main dining area, far from the kitchen window.

The sudden realization that she was eavesdropping on a private conversation brought color to her cheeks and she turned to continue down the alley. But at that moment, before she had a chance to move away, the man's voice became more distinct. A churlish tone coated his rising voice as he moved closer to the window. Po stood perfectly still, the words somehow assaulting not only Jacques but her as well.

"I did you a favor, old man. You're better off, believe it. She was a bitch." The last word was punched out and flew through the window like a ball given a sharp whack. Po stepped back as if it might hit her directly in her solar plexus.

"Out, get out of my sight!" Jacques yelled. "Don't you ever come back into my restaurant."

"Oh, I'm outta here, all right, and you can shove your business you know where. But it's not over, Frenchy. There's still more I can get out of that scheming wife of yours, and believe you me, I intend to get it!"

Before Po had a chance to move down the alleyway, away from listening in on Jacques's private conversation, a broad-shouldered man rushed through the back door, nearly knocking her down. He headed for an SUV that had been hidden behind Jacques's van and jumped inside. A shiny black Lab sat upright on the back seat, looking at Po with interest.

Po stared at the back of the man's head as he jumped into the car and brought the engine to life. Only the dog seemed aware of her presence. The fleeting glance she had as he had run past her was of dark, thick hair, prominent cheekbones, and wide brows marking a strong face. She stared at the SUV, wanting to get another look. But the car charged backward, then forward, scattering gravel in all directions. Then it raced down the alley.

The dog stuck his head out the window of the car, looking back at Po.

But it was the man, not the dog, that Po recognized. Even in the rush of his departure, Po knew she had seen him before. There was no doubt in her mind. He was the same man Kate had snapped a picture of—the man who had been standing on the hill kissing Laurel St. Pierre, blown up now into a real-life figure.

Chapter 13

Po hesitated only seconds before opening the back door to Jacques's French Quarter restaurant and walking boldly into the kitchen.

Jacques was standing at the commercial sink, his hands gripping the edge, his head bent low as if he were going to be sick. His breath came in starts and stops.

"Jacques?" Po asked, her voice gentle at the sight of her disturbed friend. "Jacques, who was that man?"

Jacques spun around at the sound of her voice. Thin strands of hair hung limp over his broad forehead. He wore baggy jeans and a stained T-shirt, and his eyes were wild and unfocused.

"Po, what are you doing here?" he said.

"I apologize for overhearing your conversation. I was on my morning run, is all, and I thought I'd stop in for a glass of water. Then I heard voices."

"Water? Yes, yes," Jacques walked over to one of the refrigerators and pulled out a chilled bottle of Evian. He thrust the bottle into Po's hand. "Drink, Po. Sit." He pulled a stool out from beneath a stainless-steel island running down the center of the room.

Po could see that it was Jacques who needed to sit. She pulled out the stool next to hers. "Let's both sit for a moment. What is going on, Jacques?"

Jacques straddled the stool next to Po and took a deep, heaving breath. When he looked at Po again his eyes were more focused, his face far older than a week ago. "Po, Laurel was confused. She was a mixed-up little girl, my Lauralee. People wouldn't understand."

"Laurel was seeing that man?"

He nodded. "His name is Jason Sands. He is my wine distributor. I thought he was a good man. He knows French wines. He travels to France.

He loves my crispy frites, my ragout of duck." Jacques clenched his jaw, the sadness that watered his eyes turning suddenly to anger. "But he betrayed me. He used my sweet little wife. He..." His fist hit the steel table, the sound rattling through the kitchen.

Po flinched at the force of his movement. It was a side of Jacques she had never seen before, an awful, powerful anger. An anger that, for a brief moment, seemed capable of triggering irreparable actions. Po pushed aside the disturbing thought and focused on the present. "Jacques, listen to me. This is important. Do the police know about Jason Sands?"

Jacques shrugged.

"You must tell them."

"I do not spread family affairs across the whole village, Po. This is a private family matter. What would they think of my Laurel?"

Po bit back a response. Her thoughts about his Laurel had changed considerably in the past few days. Laurel had wounded this man immeasurably, and his love had totally blinded him to it. But keeping anything from the police, including Jason Sands, was another matter entirely. "Jason Sands might be able to tell us something about Laurel's murder. Don't you see that?"

"Non. I asked him. He said he didn't do anything to her except tell her he was tired of her. Tired of her! She must have been under a spell. She was working too hard at the restaurant—working so hard and she would never take a penny for it! He took advantage of how tired she was, of her innocence. He used her, Po."

Po took a drink of water and collected her thoughts. Jason Sands might have indeed used Laurel. But there was more to this than Jacques was seeing. Someone needed to talk with the wine distributor. Someone needed to look a lot more carefully into Laurel St. Pierre's quiet life. She worked without pay? Laurel had never impressed Po as one who didn't care about money.

"I know you mean to help me, Po," Jacques said, "and I know people talk about me and make rumors, but I will be fine. You are not to worry."

When Jacques stood and began pulling out knives and vegetables for his special of the day, Po knew it was time to leave. He would be fine in time and being in his kitchen, cooking was probably the best immediate medicine. But on her short run home, she determined that in the meantime, she'd do all she could to erase the cloud of suspicion that was surely making his life a living hell, no matter what he said.

* * * *

A shower, fresh jeans, and a nubby red sweater helped Po feel able to face the day. The episode with Jason Sands had stuck to her thoughts like superglue, and she knew that her day was lost until something was done about it. She left a message for P.J., giving him the few scant details that she had, then loaded Hoover into her car for a drive over to Maggie's clinic for a scheduled checkup. Maybe the mundane activity would untangle her thoughts, and she could make some sense out of the morning's encounter.

Maggie's veterinary hospital was in an old house that had been completely renovated into a clinic so friendly that Po never had a problem getting Hoover to his appointments. The golden retriever loved Maggie Helmers.

"Hey, Hoover, my love, up here," Maggie coaxed, patting the surface of the low examining table. Hoover promptly jumped up and licked her waiting hand while she stepped on a pedal and slowly raised the platform to an examining height.

"So, Po, why the frown?" Maggie asked. Her fingers deftly examined Hoover's coat while she talked, probing gently.

"Too much activity early in the morning," Po said. She related the events at Jacques's. "I know you're as crazy about that little Frenchman as I am, Maggie. We need to help get rid of this dark aura about him. These rumors will begin to affect his business soon, I'm afraid. The poor man hasn't even begun to grieve, I don't think. He's still in shock."

"Do you know any more about the wine distributor? He and Laurel must have been very discreet in meeting one another. This is the first I've heard about it. And believe me, lots of gossip hits these walls between rabies vaccinations and spays."

"He must have been in and out of the restaurant often. They probably had plenty of time to plan meetings. Instinct tells me Laurel was a clever woman and could probably hide anything she wanted to from Jacques. Love can blind one very easily."

"Do you think the guy had anything to do with her murder?"

"At the least, he would be a suspect."

"But why would he kill Laurel?" Maggie gently pressed Hoover's ears wide and checked inside with a tiny light.

"That's a good question. Kate said the embrace Amber caught on her camera was followed by a fight of some sort. And I heard the man say he was leaving her, but what if that was a lie? What if Laurel was breaking up with him?"

"From what you overheard him saying to Jacques, he wouldn't have cared."

"A love scorned may say things like that to save face."

"I suppose that's true. What else do you know about the man?"

"Nothing, really. Except he had a beautiful black Labrador sitting in his back seat."

Maggie perked up at the mention of one of her favorite breeds. While some people remembered people by their names or the color of the eyes, Maggie often remembered them by their pets. "Black Lab? What did you say his name was?"

"Sands, I think. He had a Kansas license plate, so I guess he lives around here somewhere."

"Sands..." Maggie pondered the name as she lowered the examining table and allowed Hoover to sit on the floor next to Po. "Was he a big guy?"

"I'd say so. A little rough looking."

Maggie turned toward her computer and tapped a few keys, then squinted and scrolled down through a list of names. "Sands...Albert Einstein. Five-year-old Lab Retriever. Bingo, Po. They're clients!"

Chapter 14

According to Maggie's records, Jason Sands lived with his dog, Albert Einstein, just outside the city limits of Crestwood, not far from the wooded estate that Susan shared with her elderly mother. Which was the reason Po used to convince herself to drive out that way. She needed to pick up some books from Susan, and today was as good a time as any. With Hoover in the back seat, Po headed west.

Nothing in Crestwood was very far away from anything else, and it took Po less than fifteen minutes to spot the winding road that led to Jason Sands's home. She had intended to continue on to Susan's, but curiosity forced the car to turn right, and before she realized it she was driving slowly down a street she'd never been on before. Po had no idea what she'd do when she passed the house, but curiosity propelled her to at least see where this man—now a piece in the growing puzzle of Laurel's murder—lived.

The country road was dotted with new, ranch-type homes. Several houses were still under construction, indicating the area would soon be absorbed into the city, but for now it still held the flavor of country. The same address that Maggie had scribbled on a piece of paper for Po was posted on a mailbox in front of one of the few older homes on the road. It was a small, one-story house, bordered by a split-rail fence and with a large yard that stretched back to the woods behind it. A good place for Albert Einstein to play, Po thought. Not to mention that the remote area would have been a good place to shield an affair. The black SUV she had seen at Jacques's earlier was nowhere to be seen. Po drove past the house and turned around at the end of the road, then headed back down the street toward the main road. She wasn't sure, really, why she had even come.

It would be foolish for her to stop and talk to this stranger. Maybe even dangerous. And what would she say, even if she did stop?

But somehow, Po felt a need to situate Jason Sands somewhere, before she shared his relationship with Laurel with the police—or convinced Jacques to do so. Maggie had only vague recollections about the man, except that he had flirted with her receptionist and had made an off-color remark when Albert was in for his rabies vaccination. She knew everything there was to know about Albert Einstein, though, and reported that he was well cared for and a lovely dog.

"Albert is a regular here for wellness exams. He's been a patient for a year or so," Maggie had said.

As Po headed back past the property, she noticed Albert flying around the side of the house, chasing a yellow ball. She slowed down just as a figure emerged from beyond the trees, calling to the dog. But it wasn't Jason Sands. It was a young woman, dressed in jeans and a sweatshirt.

Not wanting to be noticed, Po picked up speed and continued down the street, glancing in her rearview mirror as she neared the highway. The woman was leaning over, tugging the ball from the dog's mouth. As she straightened up and her sweatshirt flattened out against her body, Po noticed something else—Albert Einstein's playmate appeared to be at least six months pregnant.

* * * *

"Po, you shouldn't be getting involved in this. You and Kate and all the rest of your friends are messing with serious stuff here," said P.J. He sat on Po's screened porch, drinking ice tea. He had listened carefully to Po's story about the wine distributor, concerned, as Po was, that Jacques hadn't revealed the relationship to the police.

"P.J., I'm not messing with anything. I am simply filling you in on things that have happened. It's what any good citizen would do." She smiled, trying to draw a smile out of the policeman.

"Your goddaughter reported some of it, too, bursting in on an engagement I had last night. She had that blurry picture clutched in her hand as if the murderer was now signed, sealed, and delivered."

"It wasn't blurry. You could see the man's face when she enlarged it. It was Jason Sands, P.J."

"Okay, maybe it was. I was having a drink with Bill McKay and Max when Kate tracked me down. We all looked at the photo when Kate thrust it in our faces. She's decided to get the whole town involved in protecting her buddy."

"Bill McKay and Max Elliott aren't the whole town, P.J. But they both know a lot of people—Billy with his campaigning and Max knows everyone. Did they recognize him?"

"I don't think so. I thought at first Billy did, but when he looked closer, he said the picture was too fuzzy. Max disagreed and wondered who the fine photographer was. But he didn't know the guy, either."

P.J.'s smile finally came, and then a short laugh as he recounted Kate's reaction. "She was offended that Bill thought the photo was blurry, even though she wasn't the one who caught the shot. I thought she was going to whack Billy with her backpack. She's a wild woman when she sinks her teeth into something. But Billy did pick up on Kate's idea that Laurel was having an affair. He thought that was a distinct possibility."

"Why? Did he know Laurel?"

"Nope. But when you're in politics, I guess you get to know human nature, what makes people tick. Maybe it was the age difference and Laurel's looks. She and Jacques didn't seem a likely match. He had never officially met her, but he'd seen her around town."

"What did Max think?"

"He didn't offer any opinion. He clams up when the murder topic comes up. If I didn't trust the guy with my life, I'd think he knew more than he was saying." P.J. took a drink of his tea.

Po refrained from agreeing with him aloud, and concentrated instead on the expression on P.J.'s face when he talked about Kate. She knew better than anyone how exasperating Kate could be. She'd been a headstrong child and the trait hadn't gone away as she grew older. Frankly, she was downright irritating sometimes. Even her mother had thought so. But Kate was Kate. And she heard the affection in P.J.'s words, even when disguising it as frustration.

"So what now?" Po asked.

"Well, believe it or not, the guys working this case aren't out to get Jacques without doing their homework. They already knew Laurel was having an affair, you'll be happy to know, although they didn't know it was with Sands. He's being brought in for questioning. But he doesn't have any kind of record."

"So they'll let up on Jacques?"

P.J. paused for a moment, then shook his head. "No, Po, they won't let up on Jacques. He doesn't have an alibi and there was documented evidence of problems in the marriage. They can't dismiss that until something else shows up. For now, though, there's nothing that puts him at the scene of the crime, nor is there any hard evidence. But there's a perceived motive, for sure."

"But, P.J., you know and I know that he couldn't possibly have killed his wife."

P.J. didn't answer. Instead he drained his iced tea, then stared out into the early evening shadows that were falling heavily onto Po's wooded yard. The trees were ghostly shapes, the brick pathways lost in shadow. The only movement was the slow gait of Hoover as he padded around the yard, patrolling his kingdom.

Po didn't look at P.J., but she felt the sadness that was spreading across the porch. She sensed P.J.'s uncertainty, and she read in his silence what she already knew—that finding out more about Laurel and Jacques St. Pierre might not be all that it was cracked up to be. The answers they sought might be far from the ones they wanted to find.

Chapter 15

Saturday morning brought clouds and a chance of rain. And when the quilters arrived at Selma's Saturday morning to work on Jacques's quilt, they brought the heaviness in the air with them. It fell on the room and on the bright pieces of fabric and pressed down on their efforts to piece together a quilt.

"Okay, so what can we do, ladies?" Phoebe asked.

Her short platinum mop was growing out slightly, and she looked more angelic, Eleanor told her, less of an imp. "But that only means you can't judge a book by its cover," she had added

"Yeah, I don't wear angelic well," Phoebe said. "But anyway, speaking of angelic, Laurel definitely was not. But what was she? Who was she? And what can we do about this horrible situation?"

"Here's what I say we do," Eleanor said. She lowered her glasses and looked around the table as everyone waited. "We rally together, put our noses to the ground like bloodhounds, and don't let one single rumor fly by us without tracking down its source. And Phoebe is right. We need to learn more about Laurel. These tales are revolting, if I do say so myself. And the fact that Jacques is defending himself about as vigorously as a newborn baby is, quite frankly, damn stupid. He needs to speak up."

"At least newborns shriek," Phoebe said, with the conviction of one-who-knows.

"Jacques came to an Elderberry shop owners meeting last night," Selma said. "And that was a good thing, I think. He needs to be around people, needs people to see that he's still the same Jacques, one who wouldn't harm a flea." She glanced at the large clock on the wall, then rose and walked toward the archway that separated the back workroom of her shop from the rest of the store. "Back in a minute so don't say anything interesting till I come back. I promised Janna Hathaway I'd show her some designer furniture fabrics for that new home she and Bill McKay are building."

"We'll fill you in," Po said. "And if Janna wants to see a quilt in progress, invite her back for coffee. I don't think she knows many people in town yet."

As Selma disappeared, Eleanor pulled the conversation back to her concern about the restaurateur. "I know grieving takes different forms but I wish I could wake Jacques up. He is so determined to enshrine Laurel as a saint that he isn't even looking at what's happening around him."

"Or was is happening *to* him," Kate said.

"It's only been a week," Po said, pulling out several thin strands of gold fabric that represented the bouillabaisse's saffron flavoring. Although she agreed entirely with everything Eleanor and Kate said, she knew firsthand the erratic pattern of grieving, and Jacques hadn't even had a chance to start yet. She wondered if she would have had the strength—or even the desire—to protect herself if any ill talk had surrounded Scott's death several years ago.

"That's true. It hasn't been long," Leah said. "But time is important. So, we need to fill in and do what Jacques can't do. And right now, that means defending him. It's clear the police are looking at him closely regarding Laurel's death."

"That's because they don't have anyone else to blame, no other clues or suspects except for the wine guy," Maggie said.

"Maggie's right. We can defend him until we're blue in the face, but until there are other viable suspects, he'll be front and center as a suspect," Po said.

"And speaking of suspects, that wine guy is a suspect if ever I saw one." Maggie was sitting at the end of the table, her fabric for the background blocks laid out in front of her.

"I think he deserves some attention." Po looked up from her sewing. "After we talked, Maggie, I drove by his house. I was probably being snoopy, but it was right on the way to Susan's and somehow the car just turned that way." She told the group about seeing the familiar black Lab—and then the pregnant woman who appeared in the yard.

"This fellow lives near me?" Susan asked.

"On the other side of the woods," Po said. "A world away from your lovely home."

"And he has a pregnant wife or whatever?" Phoebe said. "And he was having an affair with Laurel, who was probably putting the screws to him. If that's not motive, tell me what is?" Phoebe shoved back her chair and walked over to the long table running under the back windows. Today it held the coffee pot and a crumb cake from Marla's bakery. The cake was still warm and tiny flakes fell from her fingers as she lifted it to her mouth.

"The police were bringing him in for questioning," Po said.

"I asked P.J. last night what the guy had to say for himself, and he said they haven't been able to find him," Kate said. "The police don't seem too concerned. Jacques is still their main suspect."

"Oh, that's great. I think sometimes the police can't see the forest for the trees. No offense to P.J.," Maggie said.

Kate's head shot up. "You can lump P.J. right in the middle of that description. Why is it that men can't acknowledge the power of emotion and intuition? We all know Jacques is innocent. Facts…that's all they think about."

"So we'll give them facts," Leah said. She picked up a subtly patterned piece of fabric and held it up to the light.

It was coral-colored, the perfect piece to blend with other warm colors—a whole spectrum, from the coral piece all the way to velvety chocolate-brown pieces that would be used to form small pockets for the scales of her brilliant fish. "And I think the place we should start is with Laurel herself, not with Jacques."

"I've been thinking the same thing," Po said. "We all agree that Laurel is a mystery, and I don't think we'll be able to budge on this until we figure out exactly who this woman was."

"That's easy to say," said Phoebe. "But she only lived here a year. She kept to herself. How do we even begin?"

"Esther's quilt," Po, Leah, and Kate said in unison. The collision of their voices startled the others, and Po began to laugh. "I guess at least half of us agree on that point," she said.

Phoebe looked down at the pieces of fabric spread across the table. Jacques's quilt was actually taking shape. Susan had finished pinning the four magnificent fish onto Eleanor's background blocks to get a look at the blend of color and shape, and she moved Po's blocks beneath it.

Finally she looked up. "Okay, I give. How in blazes is this quilt going to tell us a thing about Laurel St. Pierre? And who's Esther?"

"No, not that quilt, Phoebs, this one." Kate pulled the pictures of Esther Wood's quilt out of her backpack and lined them up on the table.

Selma came back in with Janna in tow and walked over to the table, looking at the photographs they'd viewed the night before. "Esther's quilt," she said to no one in particular.

Kate looked around her and greeted Janna. "You know everyone, right? Have a seat." She pointed to the empty chair next to her. "We really do work on quilts back here, but right now we're trying to figure out something else—a quilt that was made in Crestwood years ago, then ended up back here under mysterious circumstances."

Standing at the coffee pot, Po watched Janna listen politely to Kate, but her face showed she was making little sense out of Kate's explanation. The world of quilters had its own code, its own sensibilities. To most others, a quilt made in Crestwood a long time ago might simply be an old blanket. But even if whatever they were doing in the shop's workroom might not be interesting to Janna, it was nice Selma brought her back. The group gathered around the table could certainly introduce her around and make her feel more at home in the town that would soon be her home. Po walked back to the table and handed Janna a mug of coffee and a small plate of crumb cake. "Selma, tell the others what you know about the quilt," she urged. "It's an odd coincidence, at the least, finding it on Laurel's wall."

When Selma finished her story, Phoebe slapped the table with the palms of her hands, setting pins bouncing, and said, "Well that's that, then. We start right here to find out about Laurel St. Pierre." She pointed forcefully at one of the photos.

"With a woman who's been dead for fifteen years?" Susan asked.

"Yes, and Phoebe is right. That's exactly where we start. It's the only thing we know about Laurel, other than that she lived on the East Coast and was poor and drab when she met Jacques. So, let's start with the quilt and try to figure out how Laurel got it. Jacques's not much help. All we know from him is that the quilt was her most prized possession. She treated it like a child, taking it down from the wall, dusting it, repairing little loose ends."

"Maybe she just liked quilts and bought it somewhere?" Janna offered.

Phoebe looked over at her, her eyes wide, startled at the first words to come from their guest's mouth. They had almost forgotten she was there.

"But how did she get it?" Kate asked. "That's the real mystery here. How did Esther's quilt get to the East Coast?"

"Maybe Laurel got it around here someplace, at some auction or flea market. I've found a lot of my favorite fat lady art that way," Maggie said. They all acknowledged that to be true. Few of them ever went to an estate sale without keeping their eyes out for something to add to Maggie's collection. In the past few years it had grown to include more than two dozen pieces—including statues, postcards, paintings, and even a few homemade dolls, all exhibiting the beauty of Peter Paul Rubens's paintings and others who had glorified Rubenesque figures in their art.

"Or eBay. There are hundreds of quilts on eBay," Eleanor said. "My niece Madeline is addicted. Buys one a week."

"Nope. Can't be that. Jacques said the quilt has been a part of Laurel the whole time he's known her," Kate said. "I think that predates eBay's popularity."

"I knew little about Esther Woods," Selma said, "which is odd for Crestwood. Her quilting and seamstress talents are about all I knew of her. That and the fact that she was married to the poorest excuse for a man I've ever seen."

The talk continued, the suppositions and the "what ifs" and the "maybes," all quickly knocked down by a single thread of logic. And all the while Susan and Leah listened and worked, carefully pinning partially sewn sections of appliqué to a corkboard on the wall.

Po kept one ear to the conversation while watching the talented artists working carefully, the pieces matching up beautifully. "It's going to be lovely," she said, getting up and walking to the wall for a closer look. "Jacques will be pleased."

"And he'll know he is loved," Leah said, nodding.

Then they all stepped back and looked at the whole of their handiwork. The body of the two fish were in place, and Po's own pot was taking shape beneath them, a design of subtly patterned fabric triangles all in different shades of black and silver and deep, shiny gray. The blend of colors and placement of the triangles made the pot appear round on the edges, a perfect boiling cauldron for the colorful fish.

"The colors will go well with the rustic look of the bistro," Eleanor said. "It's quite perfect."

"It's nice of you to do this for him," Janna said.

"He's a friend," Po said simply. Friendship bonds were a given. Something Janna would learn about quickly; all she needed to do was open her heart to Crestwood, Kansas.

"I've an idea I want to run by all of you," Selma said. She was standing beside the quilt pieces pinned to the wall. "Next Friday I'm having a display of appliqué quilts for our First Friday event. I thought I might use Jacques's quilt to show a work in progress."

"That's a great idea," Phoebe said, helping herself to the last piece of crumb cake. "Maybe my mother-in-law will finally understand why I hang out here with all of you. She can't figure out why I waste my time cutting up pieces of old fabric when you could buy a lovely cashmere blanket at

Neiman Marcus. But even if she doesn't get it, every single person who sees what we're doing will know how much we think of Jacques."

Phoebe had hit it on the head, and the others echoed her support. Selma's quilt displays were a big draw and brought many parents and alumni to the Elderberry shops, and this weekend was the college's parents' weekend, sure to bring hordes of people to Elderberry Road. And hopefully to Jacques's French Quarter, too.

"This is good timing," Po said. "First Fridays are festive, and Elderberry Road could use a little festivity right now."

"That's for sure," Maggie said, moving over to the sewing machine. "And I for one, will have—"

A rattle at the back door stopped Maggie's words mid-sentence. In the next minute Jacques burst into the room. The first thing Po noticed was that he was dressed much better today, his jeans freshly laundered and his apron clean. But the look on his face was anything but ordinary.

"Jacques," she said, "what is it? You look like you've seen a ghost."

"No, not a ghost, Po."

Kate rushed to his side, afraid he was going to topple over in front of them. She reached out and took his arm, steadying him. "What's wrong, Jacques?" She looked into his troubled eyes and detected a trace of fear.

"The police—they found Jason Sands."

"That's good, Jacques. Good news," Po said. "Maybe Mr. Sands can shed some light on all this."

Jacques shook his head. "No, Po. They found him in a quarry. Shot. Jason Sands is dead."

Chapter 16

News of Jason Sands's death spread through the small town like a prairie dust storm. Although not many people knew the traveling wine distributor, his link to Laurel St. Pierre was delicious fodder for the Crestwood gossip mill.

Kate walked into Gus's bookstore later that day and knew without asking that the small group gathered around the checkout counter was dissecting the latest event.

"H'lo Kate." Gus Schuette stepped away from the cluster of customers and greeted her. "What can I do you for?"

"Some good news, Gus. That's what I'm looking for. Good news and something to make me laugh."

"Ah, Katie, girl, it'll work out. Don't fret." Gus Schuette had watched Kate Simpson grow from a mischievous rug rat curled up on his floor reading kids' books—to the tall beauty with the high cheekbones standing in front of him. The one thing about Kate that hadn't changed a bit was her irreverent laughter and her broad smile. Today both were noticeably absent. "Looking for that long stalk of wheat?"

Kate nodded. "He was supposed to meet me here. He's late."

"Nope. Beat you to it. P.J.'s back in the history and mystery section, wouldn't you know?"

She smiled at Gus, gave him a quick tap on the shoulder, and walked toward the back of the store. In the distance, strains of Vivaldi's "Four Seasons" floated around the store. The music and the sight of an old man Kate recognized from her neighborhood snoozing in a corner chair, a cup of coffee on the floor at his side and a tattered Ed McBain mystery moving up and down on his chest began to lighten Kate's mood. She waved at the neighbor and walked on, looking down the parallel stacks, rows of shelves crammed tight with books. At the end of the last aisle she spotted P.J., squatting on the floor with a stack of books in front of him.

"Hey, good lookin'," she said, walking toward him.

P.J. uncurled his long frame and stood. "Not mad at me anymore?" He smiled slightly.

"Not this instant. Give it a while."

P.J. put his books back on the shelf and wrapped an arm around Kate's shoulder, waiting for the gesture to be shrugged off.

It wasn't.

He guided her toward a small table at the end of the row. "How did the ladies take the latest bombshell?"

"Not happily. We thought Sands was a likely suspect and would take some of the pressure off Jacques. Sands had motive, especially after Po spotted the pregnant wife outside his house."

"Not a wife, apparently. Just another girlfriend. The guy was a regular lothario."

"His only redeeming quality so far is Albert Einstein."

P.J. nodded. "That's about right. But it sure doesn't help Jacques."

"He came into Selma's looking like his world was exploding. Or imploding, maybe. Po took him home. He was pretty shaken."

"It doesn't look good for him, Kate. According to the girlfriend, Sands was going to meet someone when he was shot. Jacques's number was recorded on his cell phone."

"That doesn't mean anything. Jacques did business with the guy. He could have called him about wine or something."

"Or something," P.J. repeated. "The girlfriend said Sands was real happy the past few days. Told her they might even get married and move to a bigger house somewhere. He was 'in the money' he told her."

"But why would Jacques give money to a man he hated?"

"Maybe Sands knew something about Jacques and was blackmailing him because of it. Maybe Laurel had told him things about her husband."

"Or maybe she told him things about someone else. Someone else who killed him." Kate pushed a strand of hair behind one ear and started walking toward the front of the store. "Laurel certainly holds all the answers right now, doesn't she? Whoever she is."

"What does that mean?" P.J. walked quickly to catch up with her, watching her pluck three paperback mysteries off the shelves as she went.

She finally stopped walking and turned toward him. "I think there's plenty about Laurel St. Pierre that we don't know. She's been here a whole year and no one can tell you anything about her except she was married to Jacques, was beautiful, and stared at people. Even Janna Hathaway is making friends here—she's only been around a short while and she's as shy as a teenager on her first date. People don't let people remain strangers in Crestwood. But Laurel did. Why?"

"Well, she was busy. She helped Jacques with the restaurant. And we know she had at least one friend. She was certainly no stranger to Jason Sands. That young waiter at the restaurant was clearly smitten with her, too. Just because she didn't have women friends doesn't mean she was alone."

"Okay, I'll give you that. But other than the friends thing, what do we know about her? About where she came from? Relatives? Why did she and Jacques move here, of all places? Didn't she have any friends anywhere who can tell us about her? Relatives? Isn't it a bit odd that she seems to have dropped out of nowhere?"

P.J. watched the animation travel through Kate's body, painting her high cheekbones red and spreading out into her arms until they moved from the sides of her body and her hands swept the air in front of her to make a point. Her head moved with her words, and the whole image lit an unexpected fire right in the pit of his stomach. He fought it down, trying to concentrate on her words. "Okay, okay. Good questions, Kate," he finally managed, his tone of voice carefully modulated. "Believe it or not, we're asking some of those same questions ourselves down at the station."

"Well, I sure hope so." Kate dropped her books on the front counter and smiled at Gus. "Could you please put them on my tab, Gus?"

Gus grumbled a response, feigning displeasure, and pulled out a scrap of paper for her to sign. He didn't do it for just anyone. But long-time customers and kids who had grown up in his store could still count on Gus to send them a bill. Hell, if he couldn't trust Kate Simpson, whom could he trust?

P.J. read the shop owner's thoughts. "Don't trust her, Gus. She owes me a fiver."

"He's a liar, Gus," Kate said.

And then Gus was treated to the laugh he'd been missing earlier. It was well worth the cost of three used Dorothy Sayers mysteries.

Kate gathered up her books and turned to P.J. "Okay, now that I've helped the Crestwood PD with this slow-moving investigation, feed me," she said. "Or if you don't, I'll have to find someone who will."

* * * *

Even in Crestwood, restaurants on Saturday nights usually had a wait. Especially when they'd finally put winter to bed.

P.J. and Kate picked Jacques's partly because it was close, but mostly because they knew that the numbers had fallen off this week, and he would welcome the business.

They walked across the small patio separating Gus's store from Jacques's place and around to the front door. It was held open tonight with a heavy rock. Kate took a step inside and looked around. Several tables were filled, but there wasn't the usual pileup at the door with folks sitting on the benches waiting for their names to be called.

Jacques spotted them immediately and quickly moved their way, his arms spread wide, embracing Kate and P.J. in one giant hug. "Bonjour. I am so glad you are both here. Friendly faces."

"And good friends." Kate pulled back and scanned his face. His smile seemed forced. "It's not been a good day, but they'll get better. They must. Is there any news?"

Jacques pressed a finger to her lips. "Shhh, my sweet Kate. Everything will be fine."

P.J. looked down as his cell phone vibrated. "Sorry," he murmured to both of them, then stepped back toward the door to take the call.

"P.J. says they're working hard, talking to lots of people, following leads…" Kate's words fell off, sounding too pat, even to her, and they certainly weren't lowering Jacques's stress level. She tried to read his face. He had reason to be upset, sure, but Jacques had an unusual knack for pouring himself into the present. For calming himself down. But that didn't seem to be happening tonight. Jacques was somewhere else entirely.

P.J. walked back over and looked at Jacques. His face was serious. "Were you going to tell us, Jacques?"

Kate's heart skipped a beat. "Tell us what?"

"It is nothing. Someone—maybe a vagrant—came into my house this morning while I am here at the restaurant, and—"

"What?" Kate stepped closer and tried to keep her voice down.

P.J. put a hand on her arm. "According to the guys who checked on it—and Jacques concurs—nothing was taken. Not a thing. The lock was broken, that's about it." He looked over at Jacques. "Have you considered an alarm system?"

"Non. We never had such things in my village. How would friends get in if you were not at home?"

"Or enemies," P.J. muttered.

"It is all right. Nothing is gone. Nothing. We forget it now. You are here, and friendly faces are tonic for my soul."

Jacques ushered them inside and brushed away any more mention of the break-in, forbidding them to discuss it.

"And see who else comes to my bistro for the very first time? Our future mayor." Jacques linked his arm in Kate's and let them over to a table by the bar where Bill McKay and Janna Hathaway sat with a bubbling hot plate of escargots between them.

"Hey, Kate and P.J.," Bill said, standing up. "How about joining us?"

"Ah, of course," Jacques said. "Four lovely young people, enjoying my magnificent food. Sit, sit, sit." He pulled out a chair for Kate. "I finally got this young man to come into my restaurant."

"You're sure we're not interrupting anything?" Kate asked.

"We enjoy company," Janna said politely. "Would you like some wine?"

Randy Haynes appeared as if by magic and set two more places. Kate noticed the sadness filling his young face and realized how he must be missing Laurel, too. Jacques wasn't the only one whose life she had touched—for good or for bad.

After a brief consultation with Jacques, the diners all followed his recommendation and ordered the paper-wrapped Chilean sea bass, "light, subtle, and flavorful," he said with great conviction, "with a perfectly seasoned medley of fresh vegetables."

"So, Kate," Bill said when the wine was poured, a warm baguette brought to the table, and another platter of escargots passed around. "Looks like your fuzzy picture nailed the right guy."

"Fuzzy my foot," Kate said, pretending to be insulted.

"I concede," Bill said, tipping his head slightly.

"So how are things with the case?" Bill asked, turning toward P.J. "It has this town in turmoil."

"Oh, so-so," P.J. said.

"Right," Kate broke in, "Two unsolved murders, frightened townsfolk, innocent suspects—just your usual day at the office." She didn't mention the break-in, honoring Jacques's request. And deciding that he might be right—it could have been a homeless person looking for some food. Jacques's home would certainly be a good choice. Without items missing, it didn't sound worthy of too much worry.

"Don't mind Kate," P.J. said. "She likes things done yesterday."

"Do you have any leads?" Janna asked.

"We're gathering information. Things are moving along."

"Are the two murders connected?"

"That's being looked into," P.J. said.

"It would be weird if they weren't," Kate said. "Laurel's dead. And now her lover."

"But I heard the wine guy had lots of folks who might like to see him gone," Bill said. "A girl-in-every-port kind of guy. Maybe lots of angry husbands lurking in the shadows."

"I think the person we need to concentrate on is Laurel and who she was," Kate said. She kept her voice low and looked over now and then to be sure they wouldn't upset Jacques with their talk.

"What do you mean?" Bill asked.

"No one seems to know anything about her, where she came from. Yet she had a quilt in her home that was made by someone right here in Crestwood."

"Is that important?" Bill said. "Why couldn't she have a quilt made by someone in Crestwood?"

"Well, she could. She did," Kate said, impatient with his misunderstanding. She went on to describe the quilt hanging on Jacques's wall.

"Who made it?" Bill asked. "Anyone I might know."

"I doubt it. She's dead, for starters. Her name was Esther Woods," Kate said. "Your parents have lived here forever. They probably knew her. When we were kids, I didn't pay much attention to seamstresses. I doubt if you did either."

Bill took a drink of wine and considered the name, then shook his head and laughed. "You're right—I didn't have too many of my T-shirts custom made. But that's a common name. And as for the quilt, aren't they like other art pieces? They could certainly be purchased and moved around the country."

"Bill's right," Janna said. "My mother's decorator attends auctions all over the country and has purchased several quilts."

"I don't think that's what happened," Kate said. She paused to mop up the buttery escargot sauce with a piece of bread. "There's a connection here between that quilt and Laurel, and, well, and something we haven't figured out yet." She looked longingly at her butter-sopped fingers, wondering if Janna with her fine breeding would think it awful if she licked them.

"And who knows? Maybe Kate will actually let the police find out what the connection is, if there's a connection." P.J. took a drink of his wine, watching Kate over the top of the glass.

Kate ignored him and turned toward Janna. "I don't know if you detected our sleuthing skills this morning, Janna, but that quilting group is pretty good at it."

"Kate," P.J. warned.

Kate held up her hands. "P.J., I know this is your job, not mine. And I know you're better at it. Or at least you try to be. But I also know that the longer this drags out, the more frightened people become."

"And you also know it's dangerous as hell to be stalking a murderer," P.J. said, putting down his napkin.

Kate noticed the sharp tone to P.J.'s voice and realized that in her fervor she had pushed him an inch too far. She smiled sweetly into his frown, touched his shoulder affectionately, and said, "'Nuf said, Flanigan. Consider me put in my place."

"That'll be the day," P.J. said.

"How about some happy talk, like football?" Bill said, trying to salvage the peace.

"Football?" Kate grimaced.

"Gus Schuette showed me some old clippings today," Janna explained. "And there was one of P.J."

"P.J.?" Kate said.

"My senior year," Bill said. "He saved the homecoming game with Lawrence. Intercepted a pass and carried it all the way down the field for a TD."

P.J. laughed. "My moment of glory," he said.

"Now that you mention it, I remember that," Kate said. "You were a hero."

"Mr. Schuette told me Bill was captain," Janna said proudly.

"Doesn't surprise me," Kate said, laughing. "And he probably threw a zillion passes in his time."

"But, hey, credit where it's due," Bill said. "That was definitely P.J.'s game."

P.J. was actually blushing, Kate thought. Nice—and surprising—of Bill to bring up P.J.'s great game. If she remembered correctly, Bill didn't like sharing the glory back then. Maybe he'd aged nicely. She grinned at P.J. and rose to go to the ladies' room, smiling a thank-you to Bill for salvaging P.J.'s mood and getting her out of a mess of trouble.

"Don't forget to come back," P.J. said. His tone was softer and Kate felt his smile on her back as she walked away from the table and down the narrow hallway to the restrooms. Randy Haynes was standing by the kitchen door.

"Hi, Randy," she said. "How're you doing?"

"Not great." His shoulders were slumped and his face hung long like the towel across his arm.

"I know you must miss Mrs. St. Pierre."

"Laurel. She always wanted me to call her Laurel. But, yeah. Hey, I know she was messing with me, but there was something about her, something that just got to me, you know?"

"I think I do. I had that feeling about my high school math teacher. Then he gave me a C and it was all over."

Randy managed a small smile.

"Did you and Laurel talk a lot?" Kate moved closer to the wall, letting a customer pass by.

"Yeah, we did. All the time. She really listened to me. And she told me things that bothered her, too. Like confiding in me sorta, you now?"

"That was nice. She must have liked you. Like what did she talk about?"

"Like this town. She didn't like it here much. She was going to leave."

"Leave? Why?" Kate felt a twinge of guilt for pummeling Randy for information, especially after the uncomfortable moment with P.J. But talking to someone she used to babysit for surely couldn't be dangerous. Besides, Randy was right that Laurel was messing with him. And probably half of what she said to him was for some kind of effect.

"I dunno why. She said the town was evil or something. Said bad things happened here. And as soon as she was done, she was leaving."

"Done with what?"

Randy shrugged. "Laurel didn't always make sense. Like sometimes she talked about really nice people—like Mr. Elliott for instance—like they were bad or something. I knew he wasn't bad and she probably didn't mean it."

"She didn't like Max Elliott?"

"She hated him. She wanted me to be mean to him, too. But I liked him well enough, I guess."

Kate frowned. What an odd person to hate. Everyone liked Max.

"And she had bad headaches. Real bad. You know that one wrinkle in her forehead? It got really deep sometimes and I knew she was getting one. Sometimes when we were in the kitchen, she'd ask me to rub her shoulders—it helped make her feel better."

"You were good to her, Randy."

Randy blushed. "But it wasn't me she was leaving town with. I would have, though. I'd have gone with her anywhere."

"But she was married to Jacques," Kate said gently. "She'd be leaving with him."

Randy shook his head. "No, with that Sands guy. I told her he was no good. I'd see 'em in the kitchen together, laughing. He'd touch her, you know. She thought he would take her away. He was a bad guy, Kate. And he's dead."

Randy's young face turned hard as stone.

Kate's breath caught in her chest. She looked hard at Randy and reached out to touch his arm. "But he didn't deserve to die, Randy."

Randy pulled away from her touch. "He was bad." Kate watched the emotion sweep across his face. It was a very adult distress for such a young man. Poor guy, she thought. He had fallen so hard. And it would be a long while before Laurel St. Pierre released her hold on him, even in death. But what concerned her even more than his grief for Laurel was his hatred for a man who had been murdered. A man Randy hated.

When Kate returned to the table, the restaurant was quieter, and Jacques had pulled up a chair to their table. He was leaning in, his elbows pressed against the white tablecloth, his voice intent as he talked to Bill, Janna, and P.J.

"She loved it like a child," Kate heard him say, and she realized with a start he was talking about the quilt again, sharing it so intimately with almost strangers. She slipped quietly into her chair.

Bill was listening carefully to Jacques, his face filled with compassion. "Blankets can hold an important place in people's lives," he offered quietly.

"A blanket? Oh, it was so much more than that. Laurel soothed it, rubbed it, patted it so gently with her beautiful long fingers. When I would notice a slight tear, she would lay it across her lap, repairing it with great gentleness, like a mother bandaging her little one's knee. I think it held the secrets to her life, that quilt."

Kate listened closely, trying to imagine the tenderness Jacques had seen in his wife. It didn't match the Laurel she knew, the one who watched her enter and leave the restaurant with cold eyes, the woman who shunned her efforts to be friendly.

Across from her, Bill was listening, too, his face never leaving Jacques's, his head nodding now and then, his eyes filled with understanding. Janna had shifted slightly in her chair, seemingly removed from the conversation, her eyes watching the busboys' antics near the kitchen door. P.J. seemed to be only half-listening, too, his thoughts apparently somewhere else, probably planning new ways to approach the mystery of Laurel St. Pierre.

She followed Janna's look down the hallway toward the kitchen. Randy Haynes was still there, still leaning against the wall, ignoring the ruckus around him. He was looking out toward the restaurant, toward their table. Even from where they sat, Kate could see the mixture of anger and grief that filled his face. She felt tiny goose bumps lift on her arms at his raw emotion.

Kate met his eyes, meaning to offer some kind of understanding, to somehow calm him so he didn't completely neglect his duties. But she saw in that moment that it wouldn't matter to him. She could see it in his stance, his face. The love that Randy harbored for Laurel wasn't just a teenage crush. It was a spell, beyond the norms of behavior.

And for a brief moment, she felt an irrational fear, wondering what such an emotion could cause a young man to do.

Chapter 17

Sometimes information came from odd places and arrived when you were least expecting it. It was a chance encounter Kate had with her elderly neighbor two days later that sent her rushing off to Po's early Monday morning.

Old Danny Halloran usually gave Kate a teasing smile as they met on the driveway to pick up the morning's newspaper, Danny in his robe and Kate ready to start her day. He and his wife, Ella, had lived next door to the Simpsons since long before Kate was born. They had been old since Kate could remember, but nothing about them ever seemed to change much, not the shuffle of Danny's walk, not the pudgy, ornery face of Ella, her thin gray hair pulled back into a knot at the base of her wide neck.

It wasn't just Kate who liked Danny. He didn't hoot and holler when the neighborhood kids played ball on his yard or even broke a window. Danny loved having them around and finding out what was up in their world. His wife wasn't nearly as friendly. Ella's plump face was pulled into a perpetual frown. But she had a good soul underneath. At least that's what Kate's mother repeatedly told her, ever fearful that Ella's disposition would make her the object of the neighborhood kids' pranks.

"So, what's up, Katie girl?" Danny asked as they met at the end of their driveways, where they came together like "kissin' cousins," in Danny's words. "Anything new about that Frenchman's wife?"

Kate bent down and picked up both of their Monday morning papers. "Nope, Danny, no news." She had just jumped out of the shower and her thick, damp hair curled loosely around her ears and shoulders. "Maybe there'll be something in today's paper."

"I heard about that quilt that she had hanging on her wall, Esther Wood's quilt. Ella heard about it at the Elderberry Salon when she went to get her hair done."

Kate hid her surprise. How did that news get out so soon? But probably the police had checked it out, took pictures, maybe, of Jacques's house. Once one neighbor knows, it's all over. "Yeah, go figure." She turned and started to walk back up her driveway.

"She was Ella's friend, you know."

"Esther Woods was Ella's friend?" Kate stopped in her tracks and stared at Danny.

"Well, maybe not 'friend.' Ella's not big on friends, don't you know, but Esther Woods used to make clothes for her a while back. That was when Ella got out more, and a'course before the Woods lady died."

"So, Ella went to her home?"

"Yep, now and again. I drove her over myself. Small little place, not far from the railroad tracks."

"Did Ella know Esther's husband?"

"Saw him once or twice, I think. Anyone who ever set foot in a Crestwood tavern knew Al Woods—he hit 'em all, no tavern beyond his reach. Awful man. Even my Ella thought it a crime for Esther to stay living there with him, and she used to tell her as much. But she had no place to go and she needed a roof over her and the kid's head."

"The Woods had a child?" Kate stepped over the small patch of grass to Danny's driveway, offering him an arm to help him back to the steps of his house. It was getting more and more difficult for the old man to climb, and Kate suspected that he and Ella would have to find an assisted living place soon.

"Maybe. Straggly looking kid. Always looked like someone had just stolen a favorite toy, if you know what I mean. Kid disappeared one day. It might have been the one brave thing Esther ever did, getting the kid out of the house and away from that man, if, in fact, that's what happened. Neighbors spread rumors about it, like something bad had happened."

"That's a weird story. I wonder why it didn't make the papers."

Danny shrugged. "The Woods were kind of, well, off the beaten track. Anyway, not much was said about it. I can't remember the details exactly." He stood still on a step, squinted, looking back into his mind for the facts. "Matter of fact, Ella wasn't even sure if the kid was a neighborhood kid or lived there. Then she stopped seeing the child. Poof, gone." He snapped his fingers in the air, then grasped the side of the railing and sucked in a deep lungful of air. "Whew, these steps get higher every day, Katie."

"You better go in and rest, Danny." Kate's mind was spinning, but she wanted Danny safe in a chair before she took off. "I'll check on you later."

Danny let the door slam shut behind him, and Katie watched through the screen while he settled into his worn recliner. Then she spun around on her clunky sandals and ran over to her own house. She grabbed the keys from inside the door and jumped in her Jeep, heading for Po's.

As Kate drove near the Elderberry shops, she spotted Po walking toward Selma's.

Po saw Kate at the same time and waved, then frowned in exasperation as Kate made a quick U-turn in the middle of the road and pulled into a parking spot in front of Max Elliott's law office. She jumped out of the car and ran across the street.

"Kate, that's dangerous, not to mention illegal."

Kate stopped on the sidewalk next to Po. "Maybe. But I needed to talk to you." She caught her breath and then repeated the conversation she'd had with Danny Halloran.

"Danny gets things mixed up these days. The other day he asked me how Scott was doing. I didn't remember anyone mentioning a child living in that house. But I didn't really know Esther, so I suppose they could have had a child. I do remember Ella Halloran having her clothes made by someone. The poor dear just couldn't fit into ordinary sizes—not even the pluses."

"You're right, Po. Danny could have misheard or remembered wrong. I worry about him sometimes."

Po nodded, but she'd already forgotten Danny as she tried to stir up her own memory, forcing it to focus on Esther Woods. Had she ever spoken to the woman? Could she even put together an image of Esther? The thoughts made her suddenly sad. People could be overlooked so easily. Perhaps the woman who had created such a lovely work of art was one of them. Why hadn't they invited her to join the Crestwood quilters group?

One thing she did remember now was the night of the quilt exhibit. Po had walked over to it with her best friend, Liz Simpson, Kate's mother. The two of them had admired the quilt, then stood back and watched Esther as she stood shyly beside her masterpiece. Although she couldn't bring up distinct facial features, she remembered the look of pride on the woman's face as people oohed and aahed over her quilt. A surprised and amazing look.

Out loud she said, "Maybe Selma has plumbed her memory and has come up with more information about the Woods family and whether Esther ever sold her quilts. I'm headed there anyway. Let's see what she says."

Kate followed Po inside the shop. Her hair had air-dried on the wild drive over and now poofed from her head in a thick tangle of waves. She pulled a green scrunchie out of her jeans pocket, grabbed a fistful of hair, and pulled it tight, away from her face.

Selma opened early on Mondays for decorators, letting them wander freely with their clients before she got busy with regular customers. Several people were already there, walking the aisles of colorful silks and cotton blends and a host of upholstery fabrics that Selma had added in recent months.

In the imported fabric section, Po and Kate spotted Janna Hathaway. She was following a tall, thin woman carrying a notebook.

"It must be overwhelming to Janna, picking colors and fabrics for an entire house," Po said.

"Or perhaps watching her decorator plan the colors and fabrics. Janna doesn't look like she's particularly thrilled about it." Kate watched as the thin woman checked tags, compared one bolt to another, and held colors up to the light. Absent was much consulting with Janna, who followed several feet behind her, checking her cell phone every few steps. "Whatever happened to picking out an upholstered couch? That's all my mother ever did."

Po chuckled.

"What are you two doing here at this hour?" Selma asked, coming up behind them.

"I need some thread for the Jacques quilt," Po said. "I didn't think you'd mind if I snuck in with the decorators."

"And I'm here to probe the recesses of your memory," Kate said.

"Probe away, Kate, but know that I lose a memory cell every two minutes."

Kate laughed, then shared again the conversation she had had with Danny Halloran.

"A child?" Selma repeated out loud. She wrinkled her forehead and looked up at the ceiling as she struggled to remember. "She didn't seem the motherly type, frankly. She was so…so removed from life. Her sole attention seemed to be directed to her quilts and her sewing." She straightened a bolt of fabric absently, then began to nod as she mentally traveled back over the years. "I think maybe I do remember something now, though I didn't think it was Esther's child. A teenager came in once to buy some things for Esther. I thought she had sent a neighbor kid in, running an errand for her. She did that sometimes." She looked over at Po. "It was around the time your Sophie and my daughter Nancy were both working in here part-time after school. They knew the person who came in. I think they might have all been in school together. She was an odd duck, if I remember correctly. Younger than Sophie and Nancy."

"So it was a girl?" Kate asked.

"I think that's what I remember. But the child was so nondescript—dark straggly hair and not very attractive. No figure at all. The kind of teenager you felt sorry for, knowing he or she would most likely have a hard time in school. I vaguely remember Nancy saying something to Sophie about girls teasing her, giving her a hard time."

"Do you remember her name?" Kate asked.

"Now you are pushing the memory limits, Kate," Selma said. "But she was probably about the same age as all you kids, give or take a few years. I remember someone telling me she maybe died? I don't think she stayed at Crestwood High long. I think there was some kind of trouble, but I can't remember exactly what."

Kate listened carefully. That fit with Danny's story. She looked at Po. "So maybe wherever she went, she sold the quilt to someone?"

"A teenager running away with a quilt?" Po asked, dampening the suggestion.

"We don't know anyone ran anywhere," Selma reminded them.

A customer called for attention at the checkout counter, and Kate took a step back to let Selma through, bumping into someone standing behind her.

"Oh, I'm sor—" Kate began, then looked up into Janna's embarrassed face. "Oh, Janna! I didn't see you standing there. I hope I didn't kill your foot. I think it's these sandals." She started down at her clunky shoes, scolding them with her eyes.

"It was my fault. I didn't realize anyone was there when I squeezed in to look at this bolt of fabric."

"You're with your decorator?"

"Yes, today is couch and drapes day. I guess I'd better find her," Janna said nervously. Her eyes darted over the rows of fabrics until she spotted the tall woman with the notebook, a pencil stuck behind one ear. With a quick nod to Kate, she turned and hurried off.

Kate glanced at the fabric Janna had been fingering. It was a bolt of coarse black muslin. Interesting, Kate thought. Can't wait to see what their bedroom looks like.

* * * *

Po said goodbye to Kate and Selma and walked the short distance home. She left the shop with far more on her mind than thread for Jacques's quilt. She couldn't shake the conversation with Kate and Selma about Esther having a daughter close in age to Sophie and Kate. She felt like Selma, losing those tiny pieces of memory, and wondered if concentrating hard would help her put the pieces together that would make Laurel St. Pierre's death make sense.

She also worried a little about Kate. She sometimes let emotions guide her actions. As brazen as she was, Kate could plunge into murky, dangerous waters without a backward glance. But Kate might be on to something. And finding out how Laurel St. Pierre came into possession of Esther's quilt was a missing link that might help them clear Jacques's name.

Sleep came in starts and stops. And it wasn't until the middle of the night, standing in front of her bedroom window thinking about Kate and Jacques and quilts, that Po realized just what that link might be.

Chapter 18

"Are you teaching today?" Po asked Kate. She had waited until the sun was fully overhead before calling Kate. An impatient wait but there was no reason to interrupt her sleep.

"I'm on way out the door," Kate said.

"So early?"

"It's enrichment day. Kids come in before classes start if they're interested in certain offerings. I'm doing a digital photography class. I have about twenty kids registered."

"But—"

"I know. I know. I'm *taking* a digital class at the college in the afternoon, which works perfectly. I stay one step ahead of the kids."

Po listened to Kate's enthusiastic chatter. When there was finally a break, she asked, "Can I meet you at the high school when the class is over?"

"Sure. But what's up? I doubt if you've set foot in old CHS since Mom and Dad dragged you to my graduation. It looks just the same. Same smell, same everything." Kate held the cell phone to her ear as she slid into her Jeep and lifted her backpack onto the passenger seat.

"Dragged you to your graduation, you mean," Po said. "You were planning on skipping the whole ceremony, if I remember correctly."

"Okay, okay." Kate laughed at the memory. "But seriously, why the visit?"

"I want to talk to you a little more about Esther's daughter," was Po's cryptic answer.

"*If* the woman had a daughter." Kate answered. "I get the feeling no one knows for sure."

* * * *

Po arrived at the door of the photography classroom just as a gaggle of noisy students poured into the hallway, laughing and whispering and being noticed.

Kate was right. The smells and sounds were just the same as when her own three walked these halls. She remembered all those nights in the football stadium praying that Scott Jr. wouldn't lose an arm as he propelled the Crestwood Hatchets to victory. And the honor assemblies for all three of the kids. The art displays and teacher conferences. She smiled into the memories and tried to ignore the sweet-sad tug to her heart.

Once the crowd had moved on down the hall, Po peered into the room. Kate sat on the edge of a desk chatting with a student. She looked up as Po walked in.

"Hey, Po. Do you know Amber King? She's one of my favorite students."

"Of course I do," Po said, smiling at the teenager. "My daughter Sophie used to babysit for you."

"Hi, Mrs. Paltrow. Sure, I remember. Sophie's the best. She was my role model." Amber shot Kate a quick glance. "And you too, of course, Ms. Simpson."

Kate laughed. "Always the diplomat, Amber."

"What are you up to these days?" Po asked.

"Well, graduation—then off to Northwestern. Journalism, I guess. And for the here and now, I'm working like crazy on the CHS yearbook."

"Amber is editor," Kate added.

"Then this is definitely a serendipitous moment," Po said. "I came up here to see if Kate and I could snoop in your yearbook archives to find an old student."

"As any self-respecting journalist will tell you, snooping is both our pleasure and our forte," Amber said. While Amber's conversation was sometimes beyond her years, her giggle was pure teenager and brought smiles from both Po and Kate.

"So we've come to the right person?"

"Absolutely," Amber said. "And it just so happens that I have first period free to work on our magnum opus, so follow me ladies, and we shall snoop away."

Po and Kate followed her down the wide hallway, empty now and filled with a tomblike silence as students settled down to first-period classes.

"Takes you back, doesn't it?" Kate whispered to Po in the hushed voice the halls seemed to encourage.

Po nodded. "How many times did your mom and I come up here to find out what you or my kids were up to?"

"Lots, I would guess," Kate said. "Gads, that was a lifetime ago. I know my poor mom and dad visited the principal's office more than once."

Amber opened the door into a room filled with long tables cluttered with photos and printouts. Along the wall, another long table held several computers. "Welcome to Yearbook 101," she said. "This is where I've been living for the past year. And over there is our elegant archives room." She pointed to a door leading into a tiny room that was once a walk-in closet. "Just turn on the light and snoop away. Things should be labeled by year."

Po followed Kate into the small room. The room was mostly floor-to-ceiling bookshelves crammed with yearbooks, memory collections, and other historical documents. "Okay, Kate," Po said, rubbing her palms down the sides of her jeans, "Let's have a go at it. Sophie thought she knew the Woods girl from school so that's where we need to start. I texted her about it but her memory was vague and she reminded me of how many kids she went to school with."

Together they pulled down four or five books covering the years before and after the year Sophie graduated. "Sophie was a senior when I was a freshman," Kate said, as she blew dust off the cover of one of the books. "I remember looking up to those kids. P.J. would have been a junior. Funny that none of us can remember Esther's daughter."

"Maybe not," Po said. "Some students fade into the woodwork." She pulled another book off the shelf and flipped through it until she found her daughter's picture. "High school was a good time for Sophie—but not my boys. Scottie and David couldn't wait to move on. Kind of like you, Kate." She smiled at Sophie's senior picture with all the clubs and honors listed below it.

"High school wasn't my favorite world. But there were a few good moments here and there. Mostly when Meredith McKenzie and I skipped school for the day."

Po just shook her head.

Kate collected an armful of books and took them out to the larger room, spreading them on the table.

Po followed. "Okay, I'll start with senior year. Why don't you take the year before?"

Together they poured through the books, looking for a student named Woods. In Nancy Parker and Sophie's class there were two Woodses—a football player named Jerrod, and a girl named Shelly, who wore broad-rimmed glasses. "I know Shelly Woods—she lived behind us," Kate said, looking at the photo Po was pointing to. "Her older sister babysat for me."

Po picked up another book. "We're assuming the Woods girl was in the same class as Sophie and Selma's daughter," Po said. "But that might not have been the case. Selma just said she was in school about the same time."

"I don't remember any upper classman at all except for Sophie and Nancy and their friends. I was busy just trying to figure out why I was there." She poured through the senior photos from a year later, but the name Woods didn't show up in that class, nor the two years after that.

"Let's go back to Sophie's year and check underclassmen. If she left Crestwood, like Danny said, she might not have had a senior picture."

Kate began looking at the smaller pictures of the junior class, then moved to sophomores. Although Crestwood had fewer than 25,000 residents, it had only one high school. And buses still brought in many students from the surrounding areas, making it one of the larger schools around. Lots of small smiley faces looked out at them.

"The only class left is mine. I don't remember a Woods, but who knows? I don't remember much from that year."

Po stretched, then leaned over the table next to Kate. Together they looked at the small photos, page after page.

"There!" Kate pointed to a small picture at the edge of a row. Ann Woods, the type beside it read. "What do you think, Po? Could that be Esther's daughter?"

Po picked up the book and looked closely at the picture. "Ann Woods. Does she look familiar to you, Kate?"

Kate squinted at the picture and tried to pull the plain features of the girl in the photo from her memory. She had medium brown hair and a ruddy, pocked complexion. Her teeth badly needed braces. She looked like a million other kids, Kate thought. But perhaps plainer and more forgettable. She wasn't smiling. The one distinguishing feature was the blouse she wore. It was white, with an old-fashioned collar. And on each wide lapel was an embroidered design.

Po took the book from Kate and looked closely at the picture. "Look at that, Kate." The tip of her nail touched the collar of the blouse. "Does that look like a bird to you? I think we may, indeed, have found Esther's daughter."

As tiny as it was, they could distinguish the shape of a bird appliquéd on the blouse collar. "It's probably beautiful," Kate said. "But imagine how Ann Woods must have hated it then. It couldn't be further from the black sweaters, jeans, and T-shirts that made up my high school wardrobe."

"Well, you weren't exactly run-of-the-mill, Kate." Po laughed, remembering Kate's constant bouts with conformity and how she and Liz used to cringe when Kate brought home her finds from used-clothing stores.

"Maybe I never won any fashion contests but I would never have worn a handmade blouse. Nobody would have. It was inviting ridicule. Poor girl."

"You're right. If it is Esther's daughter, I wonder if her mother made her dress that way. Such a shame. It would have made her life difficult."

Amber moved away from the computer where she was finishing up the editor's page and walked over to them. She looked down at the page.

Po pointed to the photo they were looking at.

"That's hard to see," Amber said. "Maybe I can help—" She checked the date on the yearbook, then opened a metal cabinet and dug through it until she found the right CD. She walked back to her computer, slipped the CD into a slot, and clicked on the icon that popped up on the screen. Kate and Po stood behind her, watching the screen while Amber found the same page of photos, focused in on one with her cursor, and enlarged it.

"There, better?" she asked. "We had film of old class books and started putting them all on CDs to preserve them a little better. Now we're doing away with some of that, just keeping digital fi—"

"Oh my lord," Kate said, interrupting. One hand went to her mouth. Her eyes were glued to the photo on the screen. "Now I remember her."

She leaned over Amber's shoulder and pointed at the picture that loomed large in front of them. "Kids called her Carrie—after that Stephen King movie. She never smiled, like in this picture, maybe because her teeth were terribly crooked. I always wanted to find her parents and give them the name of the orthodontist Mom and Dad made me go to. It made me mad that her folks wouldn't do some simple things that would make her look a little better so the kids wouldn't make fun of her. I felt so sorry for her."

Po looked closer, then squinted, as if shifting the photo into a different kind of focus. She stepped back. "Amber," she said softly, "can you make Ann Woods a redhead?"

"Sure," Amber said. "Photoshop is my second name." In minutes the plain brown-haired girl on the screen was turned into a redhead.

"Now some color to her cheeks," Po said. "And even out her complexion. Maybe smooth the hair a little and straighten out the nose."

Kate stared. She saw it now, too, and knew exactly where Po was headed. Somehow it wasn't a surprise.

Amber moved a small paintbrush across the pocked face, and in seconds, the Carrie-like young woman had disappeared.

Ann Woods wasn't Ann Woods any longer. Ann Woods was Laurel St. Pierre.

Chapter 19

Kate and Po stared at the picture.

Po shook her head. "I think I've known we were headed this way for a while. But I couldn't connect the dots quite right. I still can't."

"Remember when I said Laurel stared at me sometimes? I understand why now. She probably thought I was 'one of them'—those kids who probably teased her mercilessly."

"The poor dear girl. What a life she must have had back then."

"Didn't Selma say her mom sent her away to get away from the father?" Kate couldn't take her eyes off the class picture.

"I don't know about that for sure. I think it was a guess because she seemed to simply disappear. I wonder if she ran away."

Kate was still staring at the photo. Laurel's beauty was hidden, but it was there, behind the sad eyes and the angry set to the narrow jaw. "If her mother did send her away, imagine what that must have been like. Sending your own daughter off and staying behind. I think of you and your mom, of Sophie and me. It's unimaginable. You would never have separated yourself from your kids. My mom, either. It must have been so hard for Esther."

Po's thought had been similar—and mired in emotion. And then her thoughts turned to Jacques. "Another part of this that doesn't make sense is how she ended up back here with Jacques. Jacques could have gone anywhere. Why did he bring her back here, to all those memories of that sad life?"

"You mean why did Laurel agree to come back here. Jacques couldn't have known she lived here. He would have said something, right?" Kate said.

Po thought about that, and finally agreed. "I wonder if the police know about it."

* * * *

Within an hour, Kate and Po had found P.J. He was sitting on the steps of the old carriage house he rented just south of Po's home. He wore sweats and a T-shirt, still damp from his morning run, and was reading the morning paper.

Without much discussion and ignoring P.J.'s frown at their investigative fervor, Kate dropped the yearbook in his lap, and sat down beside him. She handed him a copy of the photo Amber had doctored with Photoshop, transforming the plain Ann Woods in the yearbook into the glamorous woman who had married Jacques St. Pierre. She followed it up with a brief explanation and Danny Halloran's memory of an unkempt and maybe unloved child suddenly disappearing from town.

"Maybe this will give the police a new direction in which to go," Kate said.

P.J. was still, his eyes still combing every pixel of the photos sitting in his lap.

Po filled in the silence. "Perhaps there's a police report about a runaway child. Or something about the dad causing trouble, the mom sending her away."

Unsaid, but as clear as the spring sky, were the words: *There's a whole new cast to be looked into. The police can now leave our friend Jacques alone.*

Finally P.J. looked up. "I think I remember Ann Woods now." He pointed at the yearbook photo. "But only because you told me. I sure never looked at Laurel St. Pierre and thought of this poor girl. But sure, it's there in those eyes, the shape of her face. The nose looks like it was worked on, among other things."

"What do you remember about her?" Po asked.

"I remember feeling sorry for her. Guys used her mercilessly. I remember her sitting alone in the football stands when we'd be practicing. She was always there, always alone, always staring at the team. I think she had a crush on someone, but no one would own up to it. They'd just point and laugh. Once I heard a bunch of seniors challenge one of the guys to 'have her,' as they so crudely put it. Nasty stuff. It's difficult to see her as the glamorous Laurel St. Pierre."

"The glamorous, *dead* Laurel St. Pierre," Kate said.

P.J. nodded, looking again at the photos. "I'll need to keep these," he said.

"Of course," Kate said, standing up. She patted him on the shoulder, then followed Po down the stairs. "Where are you two headed now?" P.J. called after them. His voice held a note of anxiety, as if he didn't really want to hear their answer. Po turned back. "We're going over to see Jacques before he hears something about this new development on the news. That seems to happen these days with frightening speed."

* * * *

Jacques was already at the restaurant, his apron tied tightly around his waist. Oil in a cast-iron skillet simmered on the stove, filling the room with the smell of onions and garlic and fresh, pungent basil.

"Oh, Jacques, I'm dying," Kate said, grabbing a hot pad and lifting the lid.

"You must come for dinner tonight. I have sea scallops today—flown in fresh. Pan roasted and as round and plump as a baby's cheek." He walked up beside Kate and while she held the lid, he stirred the onions with a long wooden spoon. "To the sauce I will add bacon and cream, a splash of fine vermouth." His eyes closed as he envisioned the creamy delicacy that would grace his dinner tables that night.

Po noticed that the terrible anxiety of a few days ago was beginning to disappear, and in its place, a saddened, older Jacques was taking hold. But the chef's passion for fine food and the art of cooking was still there, emerging from the folds of his grief. It was his passion for cooking and the safety of this place that would eventually pull him through all the ugliness, Po thought.

"So why are my two favorite ladies visiting me at this hour?" He put the lid back on the pan and turned the flame down beneath it. He scrutinized each of them carefully, then, as if preparing himself, pointed over to a small table beneath the back kitchen windows. "All right, then. We shall sit."

Jacques pushed aside a scattering of notepapers, pencils, and recipe cards. "Tell me," he said simply.

Po began, her voice calm and gentle, explaining carefully about the unexpected lineage of Laurel Woods St. Pierre.

Jacques sat still, his elbows on the table, leaning into every word. His eyes never left her face. When Po finished, he turned his head and looked for a long moment out the window at the normal day. A cat stared back from his perch on a neighbor's fence, and two young boys chased each other down the gravel road.

Finally, Jacques pulled his attention back and focused on Kate and Po. "This…this story you tell explains many things," he said slowly, his eyes shifting back and forth between the two women. "It was Laurel who wanted to come here to Crestwood. Not I. No, no. She heard about this little place in a news story, she said. It was about a charming town, good places to live. 'Kansas? Where is that?' I said to her. 'Whoever heard of a French bistro in a place called *Kansas*, a place I never heard of?'"

He forced a smile. "But I loved her, and if she wanted to go live in the wheat fields with me, then I would go. Maybe she wants to have a quiet life with me in this place, I told myself. Maybe a child? But when we got here, she was different. Not excited about a new life. She was secretive here, and not social like me. Not wanting to make friends. But she was always looking at people who came into my restaurant. And her headaches got worse. I worried always but she said I was silly. She was fine. Things were good. But sometimes I would see her face go tight, and she would seem angry. But angry at what? I would ask. 'Nothing,' she always said. And…" He stared down at the table, his pudgy fingers drawing invisible circles on the wood.

"And what, Jacques?" Po said softly.

"That anger, Po, it would come back and attack me. I didn't mind. Sometimes it left her feeling better, I think, when she could scold me and accuse me of things, and even that once, she called the police to say I was hurting her." His voice drifted off as he relived painful moments with his disturbed wife.

Po and Kate sat quietly, remembering that night. Remembering the police report that was now like a painted letter *A* on Jacques's back.

"I would never have lifted a finger—or even a voice—to cause her one second of pain, you two friends know that. But she had these headaches, and I was the one who was there."

"Did she ever mention her parents, Jacques?"

He shook his head. "Only a little. They were from somewhere in New England, she told me. Her father was a bad man and she hated him. Her mother was weak, but Laurel loved her fiercely. They were both dead, she said. Sometimes she talked about her mother's death—and it always caused headaches and confusion."

"Confusion?" Kate asked.

"I don't know why. She never told me how she died. Or her father either. But one thing I do know is that they left her little money. Laurel was poor when I met her. Working those beautiful fingers off in a dingy diner. She had nothing."

"But then you gave her a home and a life," Po said.

"And it was good. She became so beautiful and so happy with herself." He managed a sad smile at the memory. "She hated her nose, so much more beautiful than mine but not right, she said. So we found a surgeon and changed it. And her hair. Washing away an old life, she said. And she would work her body into perfection at spas and gyms."

"But she somehow wanted to come back to that old life," Kate said. "I wonder why. Did she give you any hints?"

"No," Jacques shook his head vigorously as if the question now burdened him. "She would try to pretend she wanted to be here but she was sometimes rude and awful to good people—like Max Elliott, my friend."

"Do you know why?" Po asked.

"Oh, Po, if only I knew why. She acted like she hated Max. I don't know why. And then she had her...her dalliances. The wine salesman. And another man in New York before we moved. But she didn't love them, I knew. She loved only me."

Po reached out and covered his hand with her own.

His fingers quieted and a slow smile returned. "She was complicated, my Laurel."

Kate sat still. They had only cracked the surface of who Laurel St. Pierre was, but the pain she caused this nice man was creating havoc with her emotions. No matter how much Jacques loved this woman, Kate wanted to slap her. She fought back the guilty blush that crept up her neck to her cheeks.

"I think Laurel came here for a reason, Jacques," Po said. "And I think when we find that out, we may be closer to discovering who murdered her. And then we'll be able to banish this awful cloud and make you whole again."

Jacques smiled sadly. "With friends like you, and my kitchen, my cooking—I will be fine." Then he got up and walked across the kitchen to attend his sauce, wondering if a fine baby beet salad with creamy goat chevre and a sprinkling of micro greens, perhaps, would be the perfect accompaniment for his succulent, caramelized scallops. Yes, he thought. It would be an excellent choice.

Chapter 20

Phoebe decided a Thursday night quilt gathering was in order, and e-mailed everyone to meet in Selma's backroom at 7:30. They needed to check up on the progress of Jacques's quilt—and on their lives, she wrote.

News of Laurel St. Pierre's real identity had stunned the town, and stories of Ann Woods were rampant. An old newspaper photo reappeared in the paper showing Al Woods's car, a pile of rubble at the bottom of a bridge.

"Now it's clear why Laurel stared at Kate in the restaurant," Maggie said, looping one leg over a chair. "She was in your class, Kate. She was probably waiting for you to recognize her. Do you remember ever meeting her?"

"Mags, there were over two hundred kids in my class," Kate reminded her.

"That's true. And freshmen are such scared creatures," Maggie said.

"I don't remember ever seeing Esther's child around town," Eleanor said. "But I did talk to Esther now and then when I took sewing to her. I think she even came to my house once."

"The thing I can't get off my mind is that her mother sent her away," Phoebe said. "It sounds like all Esther Woods had of value was her daughter, and then for some reason the daughter disappears when she's, like what, fifteen? Why would a mother do that?" What Phoebe thought of Esther Woods was blatantly clear to those around her. Phoebe loved her twins with palpable emotion, and the thought of a mother separating from her child was beyond comprehension, not to mention forgiveness.

Phoebe brought her coffee cup over to the table and sat down.

"*If* that's what happened, Phoebs," Kate said. "As P.J. is fond of saying, we're filling in cracks with thoughts and emotion. The police prefer cracks that they can see through."

"Well, we're right," Phoebe said.

"If that's what happened," Esther reminded Phoebe, "don't forget the reason. Esther probably arranged something to protect her daughter from the father. That's a heroic thing, though an awful situation. A Sophie's Choice kind of decision."

"And how miserable that there wasn't anything in place back then to protect Esther and get her help from that abusive man," Selma said.

"Bill McKay is pushing the powers that be to get some tax money to build a place for women like Esther," Kate said. "So maybe things are changing, finally."

Phoebe perked up. "Once that place is built, we'll make quilts for every single bed and crib. There's already a fundraiser in the works. My in-laws are helping host it at their Country Club. Finally, something useful and good, and so much more admirable than many events held over there. I told Jimmy that the charity events we get invited to by his parents are mostly an excuse for fancy cocktails or to play golf. This one makes sense."

Eleanor laughed and patted Phoebe's hand. "Well, anyway, good for the town and good for Billy. He seems very tuned in to what this town needs." Eleanor sat at the end of the table, her cane at her side and a bright silk jacket keeping away the cool spring air.

"Yes, but unfortunately, it's too late to help Esther Woods," Po said. She had racked her brain for two days, trying to dredge up any memories she might have had of the Woods family, but came up empty. Except for one thing—the amazing quilt—the soaring bird and vital life that poured from the golden stitches that held it together. Esther Woods could certainly have used a friend. And usually Po and Liz Simpson happened upon people like Esther and would help out in some small way. But not this time. Esther Woods had slipped through the cracks of their lives.

Po pulled out the fabric blocks she was working on. The subtly patterned swirls of black and gray and navy fabric were already revealing the definitions of two smooth black pots.

Leah leaned over her shoulder. "Looking good, Po." She pushed aside some scissors and pieces of fabric and placed her nearly completed fish on the table. "Let's see how they look together."

"Fantastic," Maggie said, standing to get a better look at the large vibrant fish that Leah had created. It was now far more than the silhouette they had seen last Saturday. Today the fish was covered with scales made out of small pockets of fabric, each one filled with light batting. The scales overlapped artfully on the body of the fish, small patterned flaps of fire-brick red. Toward the head the fins moved into rosier tones—coral and salmon and a rust-colored pattern that would complement the textured walls in Jacques's restaurant. Leah looked over at the assistant store manager. "Susan, bring out your fish. They're similar, but in a different color palette."

Susan pulled her fabric out of a large sack and displayed her small cutout fins in shades of orchid and plum, thistle, and cobalt blue. The tip of the tail, already completed with the neat rows of small fabric pockets, was fashioned of slippery fabric in shades of dark magenta and purple. "We'll appliqué them onto the pieced background, then quilt around them so they'll stand out."

"Flying fish," Po said.

"Just what Jacques wanted," Kate said.

"We're wonderful!" Phoebe said. She clapped her hands.

"And not only that, we've completed enough now that people will get a really good look at the finished product when I display it tomorrow night. Maggie and Phoebe have some of the border done—and Eleanor, your background blocks look great. I'm going to lay it all out on that display bed I have out front."

"Great idea, Selma," Susan said as she lifted the pieces of her quilt from the table.

"This weekend is alumni weekend at Canterbury," Leah added, "so you'll have lots of people in for your Friday night exhibit, Selma. The timing is perfect."

"I should have the pot completely finished," Po said. "At least I hope to." She thought of the chaos of the last two weeks, and how regular routines and plans had been tossed to the wind. Laurel's death had been like a Kansas tornado, ripping though the small town and leaving lives in chaos. Jacques's quilt was therapy for all of them, and she only hoped by the time it was finished, there'd be no sign of the havoc the tornado had wrought.

* * * *

Even Hoover sensed the restlessness in his owner. No sooner had Po settled into the couch that evening than he stretched his golden body out on the forest green slipcover and flopped his large head on her lap, covering up the *Crestwood Daily*.

"Hoover," Po scolded, gently kneading the dog's ears. "You know better." But her mood and the comfort of the golden retriever's presence greatly overshadowed the golden clumps of fur he'd leave on her couch. Po was distracted anyway, her thoughts scattered, and the dog's presence had a grounding effect. The fact that a killer was loose, maybe in their own town,

was never far from Po's mind. Or anyone else's either. She worried about
Kate, and that impulsive streak that sometimes took her into dangerous
spots. Po had celebrated P.J.'s entry into Kate's life, not only because she
liked him so much, but because he brought a more cautious element into
her goddaughter's life, a kind of protectiveness that Kate would absolutely
deny. But Po knew it was real, and for that she was grateful.

She looked up at Scott's old ship's clock on the fireplace mantel. Max
would be arriving soon. A routine visit, he said. Some financial papers that
needed signing. Max provided in-house service, offering to bring them by
on his way home from the office.

Dear Max, whose name was being tossed around with increased
frequency in the muddy waters of this mystery. And often in an irreverent
way that perplexed and bothered Po. The thinking was shallow and filled
with false premises: if Laurel St. Pierre didn't like the attorney, there must
have been a reason. But no one was able to come up with one, as far as
Po knew anyway.

She glanced down at a part of the newspaper not covered by Hoover's
head, A headline loomed large: "Local Woman Lived in Fear and Shame."

The reporters for the *Crestwood Daily* were more interested in pulling
up tales of Al Woods's many arrests and drunken brawls and the horrors
for Ann and Esther Woods, forced to live in such an environment, than
who had killed the young woman and her alleged lover. They'd even gone
so far as to badger Bill McKay for quotes, pushing him to talk about the
development of the home for abused women and children, as if that would
bring Esther Woods or her daughter back. As if Bill McKay was already
Crestwood's mayor.

But she couldn't disparage the effort to do something positive; the home
would be a good thing. And who knew how many women in the county
were secretly in need of such a place?

Bill was handling it graciously, Po had to admit, and was promoting the
country club fundraiser for the cause. He and Janna would be honorary co-
chairs, the paper read. The event was being put together hastily, probably
an effort on someone's part to focus attention on a good thing, rather than
the sordid goings-on regarding the murders.

A light knock and the sound of the front door opening and closing
announced Max Elliott's arrival. Po pushed Hoover to the side and stood.
Since Scott's death, she had been more than comfortable to have Max know
all the intricacies of her financial and legal affairs. She felt safe, knowing
his fine mind was watching over things for her. But when he'd called to
tell her he was bringing the papers by today, she realized that, for all her

denial of Max Elliott having anything to do with the Laurel St. Pierre affair, she felt a slight twinge, a wondering, of how he could possibly fit into Laurel's tangled life. Why did Laurel dislike him so?

"You need to start locking your doors," Max said, walking into the family room. He pecked Po on the cheek, then bent to greet Hoover. "It's a crazy world out there."

"You're probably right. I'm not afraid, but the town as a whole is a little anxious, I must admit." She took Max's jacket and walked it to the back of a kitchen chair. "Maybe you're the tonic I need tonight to put the day behind me."

"Tonic, eh? I've been called a lot of things recently, but that's a new one."

While Po fixed each of them a small glass of Scotch, Max took the papers out of his briefcase and set them on the coffee table, looking through them as he talked. "I presume you're talking about Jacques's wife and the wine salesman. It's awful stuff," he said from across the room, his attention still focused on the papers.

"Yes. And what's even more awful is that anyone would think Jacques was mixed up in it."

Po walked back and set the heavy squat glasses down on the table, then sat down across from Max.

He looked up. "I agree. I respect Jacques. He's a good man, a friend. Bad coincidences, is what it is. Damn bad."

Po slipped her glasses on, and picked up a couple of the papers Max pushed across the coffee table. She scanned the numbers and read the columns as Scott had taught her to do. "There are others who had motives," Po said, setting the papers aside.

"I don't doubt it."

"Max, Laurel let it be known to several people that she didn't exactly like you."

Max shrugged. For a minute he didn't say anything, and when he finally spoke, his voice was hard. "Laurel wasn't a very nice person, Po."

Po looked at the quiet, gentle man who was trusted with more family secrets than anyone in town. As long as she'd known him, she'd never heard Max Elliott say a mean word about anyone. Nor speak about private matters.

"I know she disliked me. I'm not really sure why," he continued. "It could have been for a couple of reasons. She was rude and impolite, but I tried to ignore it for Jacques's sake, even though I didn't think she was good for him."

"Why do you think that?"

"Laurel wanted to leave Crestwood," Max said. "Jacques and I had a meeting one day, shortly before she died. He was very upset. Laurel had told him that in a few weeks, she'd be ready to move on. She seemed to be throwing this curve ball at him just as he was experiencing real success with his restaurant. Just as his reputation was being cemented. But that lady didn't give a tinker's damn. She just wanted to move on, she told him."

"But where? What was she expecting Jacques to do—open a new restaurant?" Po scribbled her signature on several forms and pushed them across the table to Max.

Max took a long drink of Scotch. He set the glass back on the table.

"I don't know where she wanted to go, and I don't think Jacques was invited, although he didn't exactly say that. But that didn't matter—he would have followed that woman to the ends of the earth. And she'd have destroyed him piece by piece along the way. That much I know for sure."

Po sat still for a minute, unnerved by the force of Max's anger. She rose and walked to the kitchen to refill each of their drinks. "We're done with the paperwork, Max," she said, standing near the couch. "Let's get some air on the back porch. It will be good for both of us."

Po wasn't sure if she thought Max would tell her more about his talk with Jacques, but the porch and darkening sky were more conducive to talk than sitting over financial papers.

For a while they sat in companionable silence, sipping their drinks, with Max's harsh words about Laurel St. Pierre settling uncomfortably inside Po's head. Beside her, Max was quiet, looking out over the grass and into the falling night.

She looked over at his profile, his straight nose and the shadow of a beard. The searching look in his eyes. And in that moment she remembered something Max had told her months before, when rumors began that the vacant spot on Elderberry Road might not be vacant much longer. They'd been talking about food. French food and his great love for it. He confessed that it had pushed him to do something he'd never done before. He'd invested a goodly amount of his retirement in Jacques St. Pierre's French Quarter restaurant.

And one thing Po was quite sure of: a French restaurant without its French cook was not a recipe for success—or for a successful retirement.

Chapter 21

I'm grumpy, sad, and starving, Kate texted to Po.

A recipe for disaster, Po texted back. At least the food problem was easy to solve. And talking might help with the other issues as well. Kate needed an outlet, and Po did too. Whoever murdered Jacques's wife was ruining their days—and maybe their friend's life. Too many things happening at once, with dozens of threads left dangling, like a very poorly constructed quilt. If it took more than the police to untangle them, so be it. It might take a village. Or at least a group of people who cared deeply about a certain French chef and a town that deserved to be rid of fear and suspicion.

Since the French Quarter wasn't open for lunch on Fridays, Kate and Po settled for Marla's and her Friday spinach quiche. The cafe owner was in the kitchen when they arrived, so they were able to find an empty table near the back and place their order without having to hear a rambling dissertation on the day's gossip.

"I see what Leah meant about this weekend being crazy," Kate said. She looked around at the small, packed bakery. Many middle-aged couples, some joined by their college students, filled the tables and booths, and Kate could see a line forming outside. Across the street groups went in and out of the small Elderberry stores, and a steady stream of shoppers paraded past Marla's, bags in hand. "We got here just in time."

"Alumni weekend is always like this. Scott and I used to love it. We'd see old friends and meet parents of students we had gotten to know. The kids were excited about summer being just around the bend, and it was always a happy, upbeat few days."

Kate took a biscuit from the basket and slathered it with honey butter. She looked around at the smiling faces. "It's a happy crowd for sure. I remember when Mom and Dad came out to UC for Parents' Day. My friends and I were always psyched about it. Our parents treated us to amazing meals in restaurants we'd never step foot in if we were paying the check."

Po laughed. "So true. These weekends are good for everyone. Merchants benefit for sure. Selma should have a good crowd tonight. And Jacques, too. Hopefully his restaurant will be filled with out-of-towners who are only interested in his amazing food and know nothing about the events weighing down the town."

A waitress appeared with two plates of quiche and filled their coffee cups.

"I talked to P.J. last night," Kate said. "He said the police are checking into everything, trying to tie Ann Woods to something or someone here. But he said from what's been gathered so far, Ann never returned to Crestwood until she reappeared as Laurel St. Pierre. Her parents' accident was so long ago, few in town can remember much about it."

"When did it happen?"

"Just a couple of months after she left."

"Did she come back for the funeral?"

"Selma's memory was that there wasn't one. So I suppose there wasn't a need for her to come back," Po said. "Poor girl— what an awful thing."

"It was. But we can't get emotional, Po. We've got a murder to figure out," Kate said, swallowing a mouthful of quiche. She pulled a notepad from her purse.

Po bit into a roll, listening to Kate and thinking about a fifteen-year-old losing both parents, living with relatives or wherever it was she went off to, and the agony of it all. Laurel St. Pierre might not have been nice, but she had also missed growing up in a nurturing family like her own kids and Kate had.

Kate tapped her pencil on the pad. "Okay, let's put down what we know."

"Writing things down is a good idea." Po looked over at Kate's pad. "It's easier to see what's missing from the puzzle when you lay the pieces out in front of you."

Kate nodded. "The first thing is obvious: Two people dead."

"Jason Sands, Laurel's lover. But according to your recollection and the conversation I overheard with him and Jacques, Jason was ready to end it right before she died, right?"

"I wonder why he wanted to end it," Kate said.

"Well, there was the pregnant woman caring for his dog. Or maybe he was simply tired of her. Laurel may have been just one of many in Jason's history of affairs. He was probably ready to move on."

"But Laurel wasn't."

"Maybe. Or would have liked to have moved on with him," Po said.

"When it was just Laurel dead, Jason seemed a likely suspect."

"I agree. But with him dead, too, the most likely suspect on first glance is Jacques."

"But he's innocent," Kate said, and wrote INNOCENT on the piece of paper after Jacques's name. "So, who had a motive?"

"There's Randy Haynes—" Po began.

"No, not Randy," Kate said.

"What was that you said about emotion?" Po asked. "We need to consider anyone who could be considered a suspect, even people we know in our hearts are not guilty. That includes Randy. He was crazy about Laurel, he wanted to protect her. He probably hated Jason Sands and maybe he even had firsthand knowledge of their flirtations and how Jason Sands used her. And Laurel confided in Randy, flirted with him, and egged him on in his young ardor for her. That can make a young man crazy."

Kate nodded and reluctantly wrote Randy's name down.

"Max Elliott invested in Jacques's restaurant. He knew Laurel wanted to leave Crestwood, and if Jacques had gone with her, it would probably have ruined his retirement savings. So he had motive."

"Max Elliot?"

"We all like Max, but Laurel, for some reason, apparently hated him. We can't ignore that, no matter how little we thought of her. And then on top of that, there was the restaurant connection."

Kate dutifully scribbled Max's name below Randy's.

Po took a bite of her quiche, then continued. "We should probably add the woman Jason Sands got pregnant—she had reason to kill both of them. In fact, P.J. told me that Sands had her down as his beneficiary, though he didn't have much other than the house and dog."

Kate added her name to the list.

A shadow fell across the table and Kate and Po looked up into Marla's smiling face. "Greetings, ladies," she said. "Is the quiche excellent as always?" She lifted her heavy brows above large brown eyes, waiting for an answer.

"Of course, Marla," Po said. "Looks like you have quite a crowd today that agrees with me."

"Those alumni folks have been packing in here since seven this morning, along with my regulars. It's good. I had a reporter come in, too, asking lots of questions about Jacques and that wife of his."

Po frowned. "What kind of questions?"

"She wanted to know how well I knew Jacques. If he argued with his wife much. And she asked about other people, too. Wanted to know who didn't like Laurel—or whatever her name was. I laughed at that one. 'Who did?' I asked her back."

"Why didn't you like her, Marla." Kate said.

"She was a pain in the behind, if you know what I mean. Bossy as they come. Always watching people, snooping around. Nope, I didn't like her one bit. None of the shop owners did. Well, except Jesse, maybe."

"Jesse?" Kate's brows lifted. Jesse and his business partner Ambrose Sweet, co-owners of Brew and Brie, were also partners in real life. So it clearly couldn't be a romantic thing with Jesse and Laurel. Odd, Kate thought. But she had seen them together a couple times. At the time she thought it was nice that Laurel was getting to know the other shop owners.

"She was always leaving the restaurant and hanging out with Jess," Marla went on. "Believe me, Ambrose didn't like it one single bit. And she didn't like Ambrose, either. Cut him down in front of Jesse more than once."

"Did Jacques know that Laurel and Jesse were friends?" Po asked.

Marla shrugged. "Beats me, but he had to have been blind not to have seen those two with their heads together, sitting out on the bench laughing like they were high school kids. I'd have thought Jesse was smitten with her, if I hadn't known better."

A waitress summoned her with a wave, and Marla waddled off to deal with the most recent kitchen crisis.

"I like Jesse," Po said. "He's a sensitive young man, and my guess is he was a good ear for Laurel. Probably nothing more or less."

"Probably. But would Ambrose know that? He's a jealous fella, Po. I've seen the look on his face sometimes. He doesn't even like it when Jesse talks to me."

"Well, I guess we can add Ambrose to the list then. And Marla, too, though I've heard her talking that way about lots of people, and I haven't seen her pushing any of them into the river."

"Portia Paltrow, what a pleasant surprise."

The familiar voice came from behind Po's left shoulder. She turned around quickly, looking up and hoping her conversation with Kate hadn't reached beyond their table.

Meredith Mellon, an elegant woman about Po's age—and Phoebe Mellon's mother-in-law—smiled down at the two women.

Kate and Po greeted her graciously, something Meredith seemed to elicit. A community leader, Meredith was magazine perfect—a blonde-streaked chignon fastened perfectly at her neck, her tan skin flawless. She was featured so often in the society pages that Po often wondered what Meredith and Phoebe would possibly have to talk about at family dinners.

It was Kate who noticed Janna Hathaway standing in Meredith's shadow. "Janna, hi. We didn't see you standing there," Kate said.

Po hid her surprise at seeing the two women together. Then silently reprimanded herself at her own quick judgment

Meredith addressed Po's unspoken assessment. "You may have heard that we are planning a charity event for the new SafeHome," she said. "I'm chairing the event, and Bill and Janna are our honorary chairs. You're both coming, of course," she said. "Phoebe will certainly be there."

Meredith Mellon spoke in declaratives. Phoebe would be coming to the country club event. The "or else" was silent but was as loud and clear as the spoken words. Po felt a rush of sympathy for her young blonde quilting friend. Meredith would was a formidable mother-in-law.

"I'm sorry to rush off," Meredith continued. "Janna and I have finished our business, and I've another appointment. But don't forget to save next Saturday evening. It will be a fabulous party, and all for such a wonderful cause." She pecked Janna on the cheek, then wove her way through the crowded restaurant toward the front door.

Janna watched her disappear through the door, then turned back to Kate and Po. "I do hope you both will come. It will be a terrific event— Meredith is amazing—and Bill is working so hard to make the SafeHome a reality."

Po watched Janna saying all the right things, and wondered briefly if she enjoyed the role of public wife. There was an oddness about her that made Po think she actually might like it. But whether to please someone else or herself wasn't entirely clear. "It sounds like a lovely event," Po said.

"Was Meredith leaving us a choice?" Kate said, following it up with a husky laugh.

"Meredith Mellon is like my mother. So no, you probably have no choice. I never did." She shrugged. "The event will be a good thing for Bill. He needs to do things like this. The more visibility he gets, the better it will be for his political career."

And that was probably the answer, right there, Po decided. Janna was doing this for Bill, and would probably do just about anything for her husband-to-be.

Meredith Mellon's event was a stepping stone, regardless of the good cause that was so frequently mentioned. "Would you like to sit, Janna? We're probably good for one more cup of coffee," Po said.

Janna shook her head. "Thanks, but I'm meeting Bill and Max Elliot to sign some papers on the house, and also to talk about another project we're considering out on the edge of town—a new, exclusive shopping center. My father is thinking of investing in it, too—he's so proud of Bill."

Mention of her father and Bill in the same breath brought a radiant smile to Janna's face, and for a second, Po thought she looked pretty.

Janna turned to leave, then glanced down at the table and noticed the pad of paper beside Kate's plate. INNOCENT popped off the white page. Janna looked at it curiously. "What's this?" she asked.

It was a slightly nosy question. But Po felt an undefined pity for Janna Hathaway. She glanced at Kate, hoping she could cut off the quick retort she could see rising to Kate's lips. Quickly, Po explained the frustration that she and Kate felt because of the unsolved murder.

"Bill said the police are making progress," Janna said, her words carrying an edge of defensiveness.

"Maybe. But they still have Jacques St. Pierre in the lineup."

"And Jacques is a dear sweet man, totally incapable of murder," Kate said, her words clipped.

"But Jacques isn't the only one, right? Bill said he talked to the police chief and they are thinking that the murderer might even be from New York, someone Laurel maybe jilted—just like she was doing to Jacques. Someone who came back here to get even and lured her out to the park that night. It kind of makes sense. And Bill said they might never be able to find that person, since Laurel was so secretive about her life. That sounds logical to me."

"But Jacques will never be clear of the shadow of her death if the crime isn't solved," Kate explained. "Nor will the town be able to move on. Closure is important, Janna. We need to find that person, no matter how difficult it is."

Janna rubbed her arms. "It's just so...so awful to think about. Especially when there are so many good things going on." Janna looked at Kate and Po hopefully, as if happy thoughts would erase the horror of murder. "There's the benefit coming up, for one thing," she said. "And building the SafeHome, and planning for, well, for the wedding." She looked down at the floor. "I know that sounds selfish, but I wish all these bad things would go away."

"I understand, Janna," Po said. "You're absolutely right—the benefit is a good, positive thing, and probably more people will go and contribute to the home because of these awful events. But we still need to exonerate Jacques from all blame."

Janna seemed to be listening, but both Po and Kate sensed her impatience. And it was understandable, Po thought. She didn't know the people involved, and she had a wedding and a new house to prepare. She didn't want anything marring those important events in her life.

"We need to bring some closure to it for Jacques's sake, if not our own," Kate said, speaking slowly, as if to a child.

Janna's distress over the murder's effect on her important life events was childlike, innocent, and irritated Kate no end. She bit back her thoughts and said, "People think that exploring Ann Woods's past a little, finding out who she really was and what happened to her in the years away from Crestwood, might help all of us figure this out."

Janna didn't seem convinced.

"Janna," Po added, "you have plenty on your mind right now, with all that's going on in your life. And that's where your attention should be. We understand that."

Janna stood beside the table, fingering her Givenchy bag.

Kate watched her shift from one foot to another, wanting to stay and wanting to go at the same time. Murder had probably never been this close to her carefully protected life. But Crestwood was a small town that took care of its own, and one person's business, for better or worse, was everyone's business. Janna didn't seem to have gotten that message.

Nor did she seem to have the slightest understanding that for some of them, concern for Jacques topped even her wedding, her new house, or the Crestwood Country Club event.

Chapter 22

P.J. and Kate stopped by Po's that night before heading for a movie in Kansas City. An evening away was how P.J. described it. Something they both needed. Kansas City's Country Club Plaza, with its happy crowds, its groups of musicians gathered around the fountains, would take them a world away from the rumors and worries of the Crestwood murders. When P.J. suggested it, Kate agreed in a half second and said she'd even buy dinner.

Po was out on the porch with Maggie, sharing a glass of iced tea and enjoying the warm southern breezes that portended a Kansas May. Hoover sat next to his favorite vet, his large head lolling in her lap.

"Hey, guys," Maggie called out in greeting. "Join us."

"Where's Leah?" Kate asked. "I thought she was joining you."

"She's being a good-hearted person and helping Selma out. Selma is expecting mobs tonight." Po handed P.J. and Kate each a glass. Kate looked beautiful tonight. Her cheeks flushed and her eyes bright. P.J. seemed to have noticed too. They both look happy in the moment, happy together, Po thought with a jolt. That's what's happening here. *Happiness.* It was more welcome to Po than the bright yellow daffodils popping up beneath the giant pines in her yard. A more powerful sign of good days to come than the bright spring moon.

"I stopped by to see Jacques this afternoon," Kate said. "He's hoping for a crowd tonight, too. And he plans on sending everyone over to Selma's to see his quilt-in-progress."

"That's great," Po said. "It's good for people to know he has the neighborhood's support."

Kate sat down beside Maggie and Hoover. "He's also made a decision about Laurel's mother's bird quilt—he's going to offer it as an item for the

SafeHome auction at the country club event. I think maybe Selma planted the idea, but Jacques loved it. Considering all that's happened, he thought it was especially fitting—and said it's what Laurel would want him to do."

"I'm not so sure about the latter," Po said. "Who knows what Laurel—or Ann—would have wanted? She's such a mystery woman, even in death. But it's certainly a good and generous thing for Jacques to do."

"I had the same thought," Kate said. "She wouldn't even let Jacques touch it. But if it makes Jacques happy to think she'd approve, that's all that matters."

"We've been looking into Ann Woods's past," P.J. said. He leaned against the railing, his back to the yard and his long legs crossed at the ankles. "We've confirmed that when she left here years ago, she went to upstate New York, so she was honest with Jacques about that. She lived in a small town with a maiden aunt, I think, and finished high school there. When the aunt passed away—Ann must have been seventeen or eighteen—she seems to have disappeared, swallowed up in the bowels of New York City. Or at least that's the best we can figure out, since that's where she lived when she met Jacques. And Jacques was pretty sure she'd lived there for several years."

Kate repeated Janna Hathaway's conjecture that it could have been someone from that part of Laurel's life who killed her.

"Sure, could be," P.J. said. "And if that's true, we may never find him or her. But I don't think it was."

"Why?" Po asked. She completely agreed with P.J., but wondered how he'd arrived at that assumption. She had her own set of reasons. If someone from Laurel's past had wanted to kill her, New York would have been a much better place to do it, not a small town where everyone knew one another, and strangers were as noticeable as blue men from Mars. Besides, Laurel's presence and behavior in Crestwood seemed to be calculated. Po was convinced that Laurel had come back for a reason. And that reason was right there in their little town. They simply couldn't see it. At least not yet.

P.J. shifted on the porch railing. He seemed reluctant to say why he thought the way he did, but he finally offered, "The dual murders, for one reason. Sands had no ties to the East Coast. He'd never been outside the Midwest and never planned to go to a big city. Furthermore, who but a resident would know about those quarries where Sands's body was found? Most people who live here couldn't even find their way down those narrow roads. Also, Sands told Jacques he was going to benefit from something Laurel told him. He knew something and thought that knowledge was worth something."

Po watched P.J.'s angular face as he talked. It was partially lit by the full moon, and the powerful lines of his jaw were outlined prominently. Thoughtfulness and intelligence filled the strong face. And kindness. If Liz Simpson were alive and sitting there with them, she'd be smiling. And she would hope her daughter was seeing the same things in P.J. Flanigan as her best friend Po was seeing.

* * * *

Po wasn't sure that Kate would make it to Selma's shop for the Saturday quilting session, knowing she'd been out late the night before. But as she walked out of Marla's with a latte in hand, she spotted Kate rounding the corner in her familiar green Jeep.

Po stood on the curb and waited while Kate parked the car and ran across the street.

Kate pecked her on the cheek. "Okay, yes, we had a great time." She took Po's coffee cup, took a drink, then went on. "He drives me crazy sometimes—but other times?" Kate lifted her brows and rolled her eyes mischievously.

Po laughed and looped her arm through Kate's. Weaving through the crowds, they headed for Selma's. The alumni crowd had swelled in size today, lining up at Marla's for eggs and coffee. "Too bad Jacques doesn't serve breakfast," Po mused. "He'd make a fortune today."

They glanced into the dark restaurant, then hurried on toward Selma's shop. The door was already open, the blinds pulled. At that moment, Selma walked out, spotted them coming, and immediately headed in their direction. Her face was tight and damp; gray tendrils were flattened against her forehead. Bright spots lit her cheeks, the only signs of emotion as she waved them close. "Not a good day, ladies," she said crisply. "I'm glad you're here early. Come." Selma turned back and walked quickly toward the store.

Po and Kate looked at each other, then followed Selma into the half-lit store. Susan stood behind the counter, a strange, sad look on her face.

Selma gestured toward the west side of the store and Kate and Po looked toward the wall, a freshly painted white surface ten feet high that was covered with this month's first Friday display—bright, magnificent works of quilting art. Then just as quickly, their eyes moved lower to a bed Selma had assembled in the store to display their own creation—the quilt with the brilliant fish flying into the pieced black pot.

Po's hand flew to her mouth. "Oh, Selma—" she moaned. The fish were still in flight, their bodies pinned on the unfinished pieced background. And running along the right side of the quilt, slashing through Leah's fish and dissecting the black pot like a sword, was a thin, wavy river of destruction—a pale yellow-white swoosh that robbed the art of its brilliant crimsons and purples and silvers.

"It's bleach," Selma said quietly.

Susan's eyes filled with tears. "I should have been watching the crowd more closely."

"Nonsense," Selma said. "Who provides surveillance for quilt lovers?"

"What kind of monster would do this?" Kate asked.

"What's done is done," Selma said crisply. She looked at Kate. "Come on sweetie, help me with this."

Together Selma and Kate lifted the whole sheet beneath the quilt and carried it into the back room. Selma motioned toward the work table and they laid it there, on the long oak table where so many Crestwood quilters had found friendship for nearly thirty years as they pieced bits of fabric together into quilts for everyone from newborn babes to newlyweds and art shows.

"I don't want any customers to see it." Selma stood over the quilt, her tight fists pressed into her hips, staring at the damage. "I should never have suggested we use it last night. I'm so sorry to all of you. Leah will be sickened."

At the mention of her name, Leah, followed by Maggie and Phoebe, walked in the back alley door. Wordlessly they gathered around the table, surveying the damage. And then, as if on cue, the air was filled with crashing exclamations, outrage, and questions.

"When did you discover this?" Po asked Selma, managing to squeeze her question into a short-lived lull.

"Not until this morning. It was so packed in here last night you could barely move. Jacques's had a line all the way down the block, and the overflow wandered around in here, waiting for their tables. Also, a Canterbury professor's quilt was on display, and students and parents who knew her came in to see it." Selma unpinned Leah's fish from the background fabric and absently, as if telling it that it'd be okay, pressed the fabric to her cheek.

"People were still here at closing," Susan said. "Leah and I turned the spotlights out over the quilts to get people to leave, so it was dark on that side of the room, and we didn't see the streak."

"Well, I have many of my little fins left over—I wasn't sure what colors would fit in best so I made a ton. I can redo my fish without too much difficulty," Leah said.

"And my cauldron just may end up with some vegetables floating around it. There's always a way," Po said.

"But why in heaven's name would anyone have bleach in here? It makes no sense whatsoever." Phoebe leaned over the damaged quilt, one small finger tracing the line of the bleach.

The room grew quiet as they tried to make sense of the damage. Finally, Po asked, "Selma, were you the last to leave?"

"Yes. I sent Susan on her way—she has that drive all the way out to her farm. So I took care of the cash register, straightened a few fabric bolts, and went on home. The cleaning crew arrived when I was leaving."

"Have you talked to them? Could they have spilled something on the quilt?" Po asked.

"I called Jake Hansen this morning as soon as I discovered it. He's the head man, honest as the day is long. He saw it as soon as they started sweeping, he said. Jake doesn't know diddlysquat about quilts—he thought maybe I had tried some new technique on it, kind of like tie-dye, he said." Selma's laugh was hollow.

"So we know for sure it happened during the show," Po said.

"Is that possible?" Kate asked. "Wouldn't you have smelled the bleach?"

"Not in a room filled with fifty kinds of fancy perfumes and waves of Jacques's garlic shrimp wafting in from next door," Leah said.

"It was so crowded that someone with a small spray bottle could easily have gone unnoticed," Susan added. "Besides, the fabric wouldn't have faded immediately, so no one would have noticed it till later."

Po stared at the colorless river. She shook her head. "Random acts of violence. It's so difficult to understand."

"Maybe not so random," Selma said. The quilters stared at her.

"What do you mean? If not random, it was aimed at you, or at all of us—it's our quilt. That's ridiculous," Po said.

Eleanor had slipped in the back door and heard the last few minutes of conversation.

She walked over and looked at the quilt, shaking her head in dismay.

Selma turned away from the quilt. She took a deep breath, then relaxed her face, a composed and thoughtful expression erasing the distress. "I think it's unlikely someone would walk into a quilt store on a crowded night and risk getting caught in such a foolish act unless there was a deliberate reason for doing it."

"Oh, Selma, I don't think so," Po said. But her words were soft and lacked conviction. Selma's reasoning was far too close to her own to offer vacuous reassurances.

"But why would anyone want to damage our quilt?" Phoebe asked. "If they wanted to do real damage, they could have trashed the store or stolen Selma's receipts, or slashed our tires, or—"

"Exactly my point," Selma interrupted. "This was done by someone who knows the effort we put into this quilt, someone who knows how much it means to us. And it was someone who knew that damaging the quilt would get our attention."

Eleanor stood over the quilt, its garish stain running down the side. Her glasses slid down her nose and the sleeve of her elegant silk blouse brushed across the fabric as her veined hands touched it reverently. "Damn," was all she said. Her gray head slowly moved from side to side.

"I double that thought, Eleanor." P.J. strode into the room from the archway, his eyes searching for the quilt between the bodies surrounding it.

A few scattered hellos greeted him, but the others turned to look at Kate.

She lifted her shoulders in a small shrug. "Okay, I called him," she said. "Maybe I should have said something to you first, Selma, but this freaks me out. You could be in danger. Someone is sending some kind of a message—"

"—to mind your own business," P.J. finished. "May I look?"

They all stepped aside so P.J. could have a good view of the bleach-damaged fabric. He looked at it from afar, then moved closer, squinting at the circuitous design. "There, see that?" His fingers traced the trail of bleach.

The women followed the line of his finger. The path of the bleach was messy, difficult to discern, like a child's first attempt at writing. And some would have disputed it, saying P.J. was reading into it, like a Rorschach Test.

But now they could see it, now that P.J.'s finger had brought it into bold relief. It was as clear and crisp as a finely pieced and quilted star.

MYOB, the river of bleach warned.

Chapter 23

"We need to talk about this."

P.J. walked over to the side table and helped himself to a cup of coffee. The women remained at the table, staring at the cryptic message. It jumped out of the quilt now, as clear as any writing they'd ever seen, and each of them wondered how she could have missed it.

P.J. walked back to the table. "The whole lot of you has been asking questions all over town. Everyone knows what you're doing. Everyone knows you're determined to clear Jacques's name." He addressed them all but his eyes were on Kate. "And someone is telling you very clearly to back off."

"But…" Phoebe said.

"No 'buts,' Phoebe. This is serious. It makes sense you'd all be warned this way. The quilt is for Jacques. And you're all making it. It's a perfect vehicle for a warning."

They stood in silence for a minute, the impact of the quilt damage settling down on them like a thick fog. Kate shivered and pulled her sweater close. Po walked over to the window and stared out into the spring day. It had suddenly turned cold and gray. Fear does that, she thought. It robs a life of color.

Back at the table, P.J. spoke into the silence. "How many people know about this quilt?" he asked.

Selma spoke up first. "Customers, certainly. Susan made a poster talking about our process that we put in the window a few days ago. In part it was because we wanted the town to know we support Jacques."

"I told my kids' play group," Phoebe added, "and all the moms that hang out in the park. Not to mention Jimmy's law firm. And his mother knows, which is like telling the whole town. Everyone knows, P.J. You know us."

"I ate at the French Quarter last night and Jacques was telling everyone who came in to come over and look at it," Eleanor said. "It was a bright spot in his life right now."

"So hundreds, P.J., to answer your question," Kate said.

"I think this act was planned," he said. "Maybe not for days, but longer than the time it takes to get from Jacques's restaurant to here." He turned to Selma. "Do you remember who was in here last night?"

Selma shook her head. "P.J., there was an army of people in here. Many I knew, sure—neighbors and friends and regular customers. And I'm sure there were plenty of that group that I didn't even see. Leah and Susan and I mingled in different parts of the store at different times. On an ordinary day I could tell you exactly who came in, but last night was not ordinary. And in addition to faces I recognized, there were all the college visitors, most of them strangers." She shuddered. The thought of the murderer being in her store, maybe inches away from her, caused goose bumps to rise on her thick arms. She rubbed them vigorously. "We could look at receipts, P.J., but I don't think that would tell us much. We sold plenty, but the majority of people came to look at the display. And a goodly percentage of them didn't buy anything."

P.J. nodded.

And they could all read his thoughts. It would be hard, after the fact, to put faces to the event. An army of people, Selma had said. A needle in a haystack, or, more accurately, in a sewing store.

He thought of Kate, and her obsession with this murder case. It was all she talked about last night on their drive to Kansas City, even though they had both agreed the evening was to get away from it all. She was putting herself in danger, along with all the other caring, intelligent women standing around this room.

"P.J., we are not foolhardy," Po said, as if climbing into his thoughts.

"I know that," he said, his words slow and deliberate. "But the person who killed Ann Woods and Sands could kill again if there was a need to do it. For whatever reason Laurel—Ann—was killed, and anyone who gets too close to the truth puts herself or himself in danger. That may have been what happened to Sands. Laurel may have told him something. Maybe he said something to someone. Threatened the murderer. Tried blackmail. And now all of you are putting yourselves out there in your efforts to protect Jacques." He looked around the room, then settled on Kate's face. "Please, back off, all of you. And leave this to the investigators working the case. Please."

* * * *

When Leah and Po met the next morning for breakfast, their appetites weren't up to crispy French toast, stuffed today with fresh mangoes and topped off with a dusting of powdered sugar and river of almond syrup. But they picked away at it, talking quietly about Saturday's quilt episode while the bakery café sounds filled in the background. After P.J. called in the police and pictures had been taken of the quilt, the quilters realized it wasn't going to be as easy to repair it as they thought. The police walked off with the section of the quilt that had been damaged, marking it as evidence.

But not to be deterred, Selma immediately went out to the front of the store and found new fabric to replace the missing sections. By the end of the morning, all the pieces for the body of the appliquéd fish and black pot had been cut and were ready for Leah and Po to work on. It was as if the assault on their quilt propelled the women, and what would have taken many hours was produced out of their anger and frustration in the small space of a morning.

"P.J. seemed worried," Leah said. "That's not like him."

"He'd be concerned anyway, but with Kate involved—and being as impetuous as she can be—he's especially so."

"Well, he's right to be concerned. This isn't a game of Clue anymore. It's a murder investigation."

"Yes," was all Po said, and she pushed her plate away, aware of the danger and concerns that shadowed them all. The bakery seemed especially noisy today, and Po looked around at the crowd. Some of her neighbors sat in the front window, and she spotted Jesse and Ambrose at the table next to them. Their heads were bent in conversation and as Po watched, Ambrose threw down his napkin, pushed out his chair, and abruptly stomped out of the restaurant. Before she could look away, Jesse looked up and saw her watching him. He smiled slightly, picked up the check, and walked over to their table.

Jesse pushed back a hank of floppy blonde hair as he walked their way. In his mid-thirties, Jesse had traveled widely, learning about cheese and art and wine, and Po had become quite fond of the young man over fascinating conversations in the Brew and Brie. She loved to hear about his travels —a Renaissance man, she called him.

She smiled as he approached them. "Jesse, I'm sorry. I didn't mean to be eavesdropping," she said. "I caught you and Ambrose at a bad moment."

Jesse brushed away her apology with a wave of her hand. "It's okay, Po. No matter. But I'm sorry you saw that. Ambrose hasn't been himself lately." He started to say something else, then stopped, uncomfortable and looking unsure of himself.

"Why don't you join us for another cup of coffee?" Leah asked.

Jess seemed relieved and pulled out a chair, lowering his wiry body with what seemed to be great relief. He rested his arms on the table and welcomed the cup of coffee a waitress set in front of him. "So here's the thing. I'm worried about this Jacques mess," he began, "and I don't have anyone to talk with about it. As you just witnessed, Ambrose blows up when I mention it. But I need to talk—" He looked at Po, then Leah, his brown eyes sad. "You know?"

They didn't know, but nodded, encouraging Jesse to go on. "We heard about your quilt today," he said. "Another awful piece to this puzzle."

"You heard about the damage?" Po said. She was surprised and not surprised. The Elderberry neighborhood was tight, and the news of something happening in Selma's shop was bound to leak out.

Jesse nodded. "Marla told us. Ambrose and I were talking with Billy McKay and his fiancée." He nodded to a table on the other side of the room where Bill and Janna were having breakfast with the Reverend Gottrey and his wife.

"Marla was upset. And then Billy got upset, too. Real upset. Turned red in the face. That kind of upset. People care about all of you quilting friends."

"It's an uneasy time, Jesse," Po said. "How are you doing with all of this? Is it affecting your business at all?" Po knew she was giving him an out to talk about something less personal, even though that wasn't what she cared to hear about. Nor did she suspect it was what was causing the young man such distress. But she wanted Jesse to feel safe, and then he would tell them what was upsetting him so. Or not.

Jesse looked away, as if collecting his thoughts, not knowing how much he wanted to say. Finally, he looked back to the two calm, kindly women and spoke softly. "I loved Laurel St. Pierre. A sweet person emerged from beneath all that anger that defined her.

"I know how awful she could be. I know she hurt Jacques and hated some people in this town, but it was almost as if there were two people inside her." His eyes filled as he talked. "I don't know how I loved her, if you know what I mean. That's confusing to me. But I know she was a part of my soul. And the thought that someone could have murdered that special flower blooming inside her is hard to come to grips with."

Po felt an unexpected rush of compassion for him. Whether Laurel's affection for him had been real or fabricated didn't even matter. It had been real to him. "This must be terribly difficult for you. But I have a question. I'm surprised that Laurel hated people in Crestwood. That's such a strong word—hate—and I didn't think she even knew that many people. Whom did she know well enough to hate?"

"Laurel didn't need to know people well to hate them, Po. If they crossed her—like Ambrose did—or did anything that offended her, she would cross them off her list."

"How did Ambrose cross Laurel?"

"He didn't really cross her. He snubbed her. He had seen her be rude to people and simply reciprocated. He wouldn't wait on her in the store. But really..." Jesse paused. Then he finished his thought. "Ambrose could see my affection for her. He was jealous, plain and simple. He has a problem with that, even though my friendship with Laurel didn't affect my love for him."

"That's difficult. Jealousy is an ugly thing," Leah said.

Jesse nodded, then smiled. "He's getting better. But it wasn't just Ambrose she didn't like—he was a minor irritant to her. There were some people in town that she reserved a real strong distaste for. I never understood why. She'd only say that her life would have been different if they hadn't messed with it."

"Do you have any idea who she was she talking about?" Leah asked.

Jesse shrugged. "Don't really know. She said I didn't need to know. It only mattered that her life had been ruined by people who lived here. It didn't make sense at all because she never told me she had lived here when she was younger. That sheds new light on everything. But I still don't know why she hated people or why she would have come back here." He drained his coffee cup and sat back in the chair. "She'd been really hurt. But she'd never be hurt again, she said. Now she'd be the one doing the hurting. When she talked like that, her eyes turned black and she looked like another person. Almost witch-like," Jesse said, his voice nearly a whisper, as if he could see her standing there in front of him. "It'd be as if she were alone, and she'd mutter to herself. 'No more hatchet jobs,' she'd say."

Chapter 24

Kate blew a soap bubble from her bare arm and continued scrubbing the large pot. "How sad. Jesse is a sweet man. Laurel probably sensed that he was somehow safe. But I still have trouble squaring the Laurel I knew with the one that Jesse loved." She handed the pot to Maggie to dry.

Po nodded. She understood. But when Jesse had talked about Laurel, his feelings made sense.

It was late, supper had lasted longer than usual, and most of their friends had left. Po, Kate, and Maggie Helmers were alone in the kitchen, finishing up the last of the cooking utensils. And Po was finishing up her retelling of the conversation she'd had with Jesse

"It almost makes me wish I had known Laurel better and had seen that side of her," Maggie said. "Though I mostly only get to know people with dogs and cats."

"Leah had the same regret about not getting to know her," Po said. "Laurel came close to talking to her a couple of times, and now she wishes she'd encouraged it. Maybe it would have provided her with an outlet. Poor Jesse seemed to be one of the few people she confided in."

"And Jason Sands," Maggie said.

"But that was different. That wasn't friendship. Jacques said there'd been others like Jason. Some women have a knack for picking abusive, awful men." Po wiped her hands and sat down at the kitchen table, watching Maggie and Kate finish the last few pots.

"Sands was like her father," Kate said. "Some women do that. Abused once, they seem to look for the same kind of man." She wiped dry a giant platter that had held a whole salmon hours earlier.

Po sipped a cup of Sleepy Time tea, her mind revisiting a medley of conversations over the course of the day and evening. "Jacques certainly didn't fit that abusive mold, but I think Laurel picked him for other reasons."

"He probably gave her security," Maggie said.

"And he gave her what she needed to return to Crestwood on her own terms. He'd have done anything she asked." Po said.

"That comment that Jesse repeated, what was it, something about a hatchet? That's a strange thing for Laurel to say," Kate said.

Po and Maggie agreed. They sat in silence for a few minutes, their bodies weary from a long day, but their minds alive with a puzzle they couldn't solve. Gus and Rita Schuette had brought Jacques to supper—a welcome surprise. He had lost some weight, but in the company of friends, he'd relaxed and even had seconds on the sesame-marinated salmon that P.J. had prepared on the grill.

Everyone assiduously avoided the events filling the papers and rumor mill, and conversation had turned to lighter things, including Meredith Mellon's gala event coming up the next Saturday night.

"You will all come, please?" Jacques had asked, and without missing a beat, they'd all agreed to attend an event that none of those present rated high on their "must do" lists. Country club galas were few and far between. But for Jacques, they would dress up, and smile, and be there on time.

Now, in the comfort of Po's kitchen with defenses down, Kate questioned their universal response. "Here's mine. I'd rather scrub your grill, Po." She pulled on her jean jacket and looked around the kitchen for her bag. "I will happily donate to SafeHome. It's a great project for a good cause—and Janna and Billy are generous in helping—but dressing up and being gracious and upbeat right now is like climbing Mount Everest in a bikini."

"It's four hours out of our week. We can do this for Jacques. Auctioning off Laurel's quilt to strangers is quite a gesture—it's the one meaningful thing of Laurel's that he owns. He keeps saying that the quilt was her whole life. It won't be easy for him."

Kate nodded. "I know, I know. And Phoebe's thrilled she won't be there by herself. I'm finished complaining about it. For now."

"Let's just hope by next Saturday we can enjoy ourselves and not be looking over our shoulders to see if there's someone lurking in the shadows or spraying bleach on our clothes," Maggie said. She grabbed the keys to her truck and headed for the back door.

Kate agreed. "I guess that would be worthy of a celebration, even if it meant hanging out at Mrs. Mellon's country club."

But her words drifted off as all three of the women wondered wearily if a charity event at a country club could even make a dent in the drama that surrounded Jacques St. Pierre.

* * * *

Kate taught at Crestwood High most of the next week. Sandy Kindred, a teacher who'd taught Kate Honors English when she was a student at Crestwood High, had started requesting Kate as her substitute teacher when she couldn't be there. And Kate was finding she liked the regularity of teaching the same class every day. She could be more than a body in the room handing out worksheets.

Kate spent the week caught up in an eerie whirl of reminiscences as she walked the halls of her old school. Although she'd been around the school for over a year now, this week was different. She knew it was because of Ann Woods. Another student who had sat in the same chairs and taken tests on the same desks.

The halls were still familiar, with that distinctive odor, and she felt herself walking them today, not as Kate Simpson, teacher—but as Kate, the freshman, determined not to let any upperclassman get the better of her, determined to be her own person.

She paused in front of the giant bulletin board outside the gym, crammed with final school year notices, pages curling up at the corners and a few scribbles added by passersby.

WIN WITH FLYNN FOR CLASS PRESIDENT signs, and posters urging the soccer team on to the state finals. GO HATCHETS! they screamed in giant neon letters.

Kate stared at the signs and notices and wondered how many times she had passed Ann Woods in this very spot and never said hi, or even nodded at her.

As the week went on, Kate attacked the shadows of her memory at every change of class, every student announcement, trying to pull back the past. Some events slowly surfaced, but they were cloudy, thin memories of things like senior boys knocking into someone who might have been Ann, teasing her, flirting with her with macho arrogance, then laughing behind her back.

Even patting her inappropriately. They'd be sued for sexual harassment today, Kate thought.

On Friday, Kate walked into the teacher's lounge during her free period. She was exhausted for no earthly reason and was ready for the week to end. Betsy Carroll sat on the old sofa at the far end of the lounge, reading a book, her glasses perched on the end of her long nose. She still looked the same to Kate—the wise and even-tempered counselor who had done her best to keep Kate out of trouble when she was a student. And when that failed, she had helped her out of her messes. Kate loved the easy friendship that had evolved in recent months as they got to know each other again, this time as peers.

Betsy looked up as Kate walked over. She smiled and dropped her book on her lap, patting the cushion next to her.

"Flop before you drop, Kate."

Kate grabbed a bottle of water from the small refrigerator and sat down next to Betsy.

"What's up?" Betsy asked, sliding her glasses to the top of her head. "You've been distracted all week. I see you staring into empty spaces and seeing someone there. Or something."

"You haven't lost that crazy ability to see inside people's heads, have you?" She wasn't sure herself what was going on inside her head. It was an uncomfortable nagging, the pea beneath the princess's mattress. "It's this whole Ann Woods thing, Betsy. Being back here like this, knowing she and I walked these halls together, maybe sat through old Mrs. Aldrich's algebra class or Goldie Bacon's gym class—and I don't remember it. Don't remember *her*, except vaguely, and for the awful things. Guys teasing her in the cafeteria, girls making fun of her homemade clothes, all that bad stuff. And I keep thinking that if I could remember more, maybe I could put it to rest. Somehow."

"No one knew Ann Woods very well, Kate."

"Do you remember her?"

"I didn't know Laurel St. Pierre, except to see her in the restaurant occasionally, and I never connected the two women. But yes, I remember Ann. She was one of my students, just like you were."

"So you counseled her."

"I tried to. Ann didn't talk much, but she started to open up a little at the end." Betsy frowned, then turned her head and looked out the window.

Kate followed her gaze. Students drifted out onto the sprawling lawn in front of the school, an art class gathering to sketch the giant elms that shaded the circle drive. It was all so peaceful. Nothing like Ann Woods's time at Crestwood had been.

Betsy turned back. "You knew that Ann never finished her freshman year, didn't you?"

Kate nodded. "We heard she went to New York State and lived with an aunt."

"I tried to talk her parents out of that. I thought they were doing it just because Ann was having a hard time, being teased and such. I thought if I could just talk to the parents and get her some help, teach her some social skills, help her to dress nicely and fit in a little more, that maybe things would be better for her. I think she wanted to fit in. She hated the teasing. She was starting to be interested in things around here. She even had a crush on one of the boys on the football team. Normal things. I thought maybe we could work it all out. Help her through the difficult teen times."

"But her parents thought differently?"

"They wouldn't even talk to me. Never answered my calls. One day Ann was here, looking sickly and sad. She signed the appointment sheet to talk to me. But she didn't show up that afternoon. And the next day she was gone."

"And you never saw her again?"

"Once—the day after she dropped out of school. I was coming back from a meeting that night and stopped in at Wally's drugstore over near the river. Ann was on the payphone outside, yelling at someone on the other end of the phone. She was sobbing and yelling, all at the same time. It was frightening."

"Who was she talking to?"

"It was a guy. I heard her tell him she hated him. That her life was ruined. And she told the person that she thought he loved her. And then she dropped the phone and folded up on the floor of the phone booth like a little girl, sobbing as if she were going to die. My heart nearly broke at the sight of her."

"Did she see you?"

Betsy nodded. "She looked up at me, and Kate, I've never seen such sadness. But it was mixed with an anger that I could feel in her thin arms as I helped her to her feet."

"And that was it?"

"Almost. A car pulled up then, nearly running onto the sidewalk. It was that drunken father of hers. He leaned out the car window and yelled for her to get in the car. And then he cursed at her, called her names, and mumbled things that didn't make any sense."

"What did he say?"

"He told her that at least this time he would get something back from all the trouble she had caused. He'd make a pretty penny off her getting knocked up, he said, and he'd get rid of her as part of the bargain. His words were slurred, but his message was clear.

"Ann stumbled over to the car and he drove off before she had even closed the door."

Chapter 25

"Ann Woods was pregnant?" Kate sat frozen on the couch. For all the bad thoughts she'd had about Laurel St. Pierre, she felt herself drowning in emotion for a fifteen-year-old girl who'd found herself pregnant, alone, and was then disowned and sent down the river by a drunken father.

"Yes, I think so. His words certainly indicated it. And I had suspected it about a week before all that happened. She wasn't feeling very good, and she came to me to be excused from gym. The nurse was overloaded so sometimes counselors filled in with those sorts of permissions back then. She didn't tell me she was pregnant, but for the first time since I'd known her, she seemed oddly happy. As if something good was happening in her life."

"She was happy to be pregnant?"

"I think so, but of course I wasn't sure that's what it was. I suggested she might have the flu, and that she should go home and rest. But she insisted she was fine, though she was making steady trips to the bathroom in my office. The walls are thin—I knew she was sick."

Kate wrapped her arms around herself, suddenly chilled. *Pregnant.* But what could have happened to the child? She'd be, what, twelve now? She thought about Jacques and wondered if any of this had been shared with him.

"I watched her that week, coming to school each day, with a certain glow about her. But each day she seemed a little less sure of herself, more cautious. And then, like I said before, she came in one morning looking like her life was about to end, and the next day she was gone."

"So, she was sent away because she was pregnant, not because her mother was trying to get her away from her father, which was what we all thought."

Betsy nodded. "The poor girl didn't have much of a chance. Her mother loved her, but she was no match for Al Woods."

"Meeting Jacques was the best thing that ever happened to Laurel," Kate said. "That was a chance."

Betsy agreed, but added wisely, "A lot had happened to Ann before she met Jacques. And those things surely shaped the woman she had become. So what she brought to their relationship, why she married him, all of those things were affected by what happened to her right here at Crestwood High. And probably continued."

Kate got up and put her bottle in the recycling bin.

"Betsy," she said, turning back to her mentor and friend. "Do you know who the father was?"

Betsy put her book into her purse and rose from the couch. "No, I thought about it, wondered about it, but I never knew. There was talk in the teachers' lounge and around school after she left, some rumblings about the crushes she had, and how boys had led her on. But no one had ever seen her with a boy in what you'd consider a relationship. Ann wasn't the kind of girl the kids paid much attention to—you probably don't even remember when she disappeared from your class."

Kate nodded slowly. That was absolutely right. She didn't notice her absence, except for maybe a fleeting awareness. And she hadn't noticed her presence much, either. Carrie, as the older kids called her, the girl with the weird hair and clothes, was all that rang in her head, and the thought made Kate immeasurably sad.

* * * *

Since the quilters had met during the week and most of them would be going to the party that night at the country club, the Saturday quilting session at Selma's was cancelled for the day. Kate jogged over to Po's and the two sat together at the kitchen table, drinking cups of strong coffee. They sat in silence, absorbing the sadness that was Ann Woods's life, and feeling like they needed to grieve for Laurel St. Pierre a second time.

"It's beginning to make a frightening kind of sense," Kate said, her eyes following a robin as it perched briefly on a branch, then flew off to its nest.

After leaving school the day before, Kate bought an apple pie at Marla's and took it over to Danny Halloran's home. Ella Halloran's memory was a peculiar thing—some days she barely knew who Kate was, but she could tell her what she ate for dinner on her and Danny's wedding day fifty years earlier. Friday was one of those days. Ella remembered Esther Woods as clear as a Kansas sky.

In starts and stops, Ella told Kate about Ann Woods leaving town. She remembered it, because Esther and that no-good husband of hers up and moved to a bigger house right after the girl left. Seemed so odd, Ella said, that they'd wait until there were only two of them, then move to a big, fancy house. "And shortly after that, right after Esther finished sewing a pink brocade suit with mother-of-pearl buttons for me to wear to the garden club's spring luncheon, she stopped sewing," Ella said. "Didn't need the money, I suppose.

"But not a month or so after, when she might finally have had some leisure time, her drunken galoot of a husband killed them both in that bloody car wreck."

"How much tragedy can one family bear?" Po said. But the thought of the Woodses moving to a better neighborhood so shortly after their child left wiped away some of the sympathy.

"I'm almost sure Jacques never knew about the baby," Po said softly. Kate's news had jarred her. She had built up many scenarios in her mind, but this hadn't been one of them. She knew Ann Woods had been hurt, she knew Laurel wanted revenge. But the thought of a baby in the middle of it had not occurred to her. "Jacques told me once that Laurel couldn't have children. It was one of the great sorrows of their life, he said."

"What do you think happened to the baby? I wonder if the father raised it."

Though she had no reason to conjecture, Po didn't think that was the case. More likely the boy who got her pregnant was the one on the phone that night, telling Ann to get lost, get out of his life. They were just kids. Besides, the child would have been born on the East Coast, the father probably still in high school in the Midwest.

The pieces were slowly coming together and Po almost wished she could stop it. It was a giant ball rolling down the hill, and Po was afraid of what would happen when it crashed at the bottom and all the secrets fell out. "Kate," she asked suddenly, lifting her head as an idea made its way into her head, "Did Ella Halloran ever mention where Al Woods worked?"

"He did construction work. It irritated Ella terribly—as if it were any of her business. But she said he'd come into the house while she was there for fittings and he wouldn't have showered. He tracked mud all over the small house and smelled awful, she said. And then he'd sit at the kitchen table and drink beer in his soiled T-shirt. Made her sick, she said."

Po stood and walked over to a small mirror in the kitchen. She ran a brush through her hair, then slid a light lipstick across her lips and swept blush across her cheekbones, avoiding the woman looking back at her from the mirror, that wise part of her soul who would have told her to mind her own business.

"Kate," she said abruptly, turning away from the mirror and grabbing a jean jacket from the back of her chair, "Let me give you a ride home. I know you have things to do to get ready for the party tonight, and I've a slew of errands to run. Find something lovely to wear tonight, and how about if you and P.J. pick me up at eight?"

* * * *

Po's trip to the library was brief. Ten minutes with the newspaper obituary records told her all she needed to know about the tragic accident of Esther and Al Woods and their funeral. There was one child, the obit read, who now lived on the East Coast. Neither the name nor gender was mentioned. The newspaper article relating the accident was a little more detailed and chatty, as small-town journalism sometimes is. It told how Al and Esther had attended a company picnic that afternoon, and Al had consumed a tremendous quantity of beer. His blood alcohol level, the article said, was four times the legal limit. At the time of the accident, they were driving back to a home that had recently been purchased on a hill just outside town. There was a question about the brakes on Al Woods's new truck, but the weaving that had been viewed by several witnesses made that less important than the fact that Al was very drunk.

And, Po thought, there was no family to force an investigation, so it was probably not even attended to. The funeral was private, the article read, as the couple had wished, and the bodies would be cremated. United Quarry had set up a memorial fund with the proceeds to go to Mothers Against Drunk Drivers. Generous company, Po thought. When Scott died, the college had set up a scholarship fund in his name, and Po was touched by the gesture and knew it would have been just what he wanted. Each year a deserving student was able to attend Canterbury College—and Scott was thought of and honored as the generous, lovely man he was.

The memorial fund for Al Woods was another matter. But if it benefited a good cause, Po was for it. On a whim, she typed the words UNITED QUARRY into her search engine, and in an instant, the screen listed pages of newspaper articles detailing the successful company that had its beginnings in Crestwood and now did business in Florida as well. On the home page, Po read about the company's magnanimous giving to charities and political campaigns. She clicked on the ABOUT US button and scanned the names listed on the page—the board of directors and founders and staff—looking for familiar names. Max Elliott was there, which was no surprise to her. Max was everywhere, a silent, respectable member of more boards and charities than Po could count. Po read on, and then stopped suddenly, her eyes settling on another familiar name.

"Of course," she said out loud. "I should have remembered that." She stopped reading the screen, and looked off into the events of the past few weeks, her heart pounding in her chest. Scott had delighted in her overactive imagination. A necessary tool for a writer, he had said. And maybe that's exactly what she was doing now. Writing fiction in her head. Or were the jagged pieces of this puzzle starting to fit together in a way Po couldn't have imagined just a short time ago?

She picked her purse up from the floor and walked slowly out of the library, thinking sadly about Ann Woods, and how her life might truly have been different.

Chapter 26

Po took a deep pink beaded sweater out of her closet and pulled it over her head, then stepped into a long black skirt and fastened it in the back, barely noticing if the two pieces matched. Dressing for a fancy charity event was the furthest thing from her mind.

Thoughts of Jacques ran through her head, and of all the people who had rallied around him. She dug through her jewelry box and pulled out a chunky rose quartz necklace—a gift from Scott. One of those no-special-day gifts that he sometimes surprised her with.

Why are you on my mind so much today, dear Scott?

She fingered the necklace and looked around, as if Scott Paltrow would suddenly materialize right behind her, and she could talk all this over with him, listen to his wise words, hearing the caution in his voice. She had no proof for her suspicions, just a bunch of isolated facts that seemed to converge uncomfortably on the same bumpy road.

Po looked in the mirror and fastened the necklace around her neck. She'd see Max tonight. Maybe he could help. He was an important link in the whole mess, and for an awful reason: he was one of the people the adult Ann Woods hated.

The sound of P.J.'s car in the drive pushed the thoughts into the shadows of her mind and she managed to put a smile in place. This was a special night. Jacques needed them all there as he gave his quilt away to a good cause.

Po lifted a soft black shawl from the back of her bedroom chair and hurried downstairs to her waiting ride.

* * * *

The Crestwood Country Club was west of town, built along the grassy banks of the Emerald River. A golf course wrapped around the property and touched close to the water in places, making it a challenging and energizing course. And down the carefully manicured drive from the main clubhouse, stables housed championship steeds, riding horses, and several show horses owned by members.

Po, P.J., and Kate drove up the long drive to the clubhouse. Low gaslights along the way flickered against the dark night. A breeze ruffled the newly leafed-out branches of pear and cherry trees and in the distance, the sounds of strings floated into the night air.

The drive to the club had been a quiet one. Po sat in the back, alone with her thoughts. But she noticed the pensive look on both Kate's and P.J.'s faces, and she wondered briefly if they were all thinking the same thoughts, each in their own way, treading the same minefield. Thoughts that would eventually emerge more fully formed and become real. There was something safe about keeping them inside your head. Just like writing a book, she thought. Safe inside, they could still be manipulated and changed. And they couldn't hurt anyone.

Sadly, life wasn't so easily edited or protected.

Po looked up at the well-lit clubhouse. It sparkled with life and gaiety. Tonight would be happy. Tonight they would put aside worries and suspicions and uncomfortable thoughts and be there for Jacques. Tomorrow would come soon enough.

P.J. pulled into a parking spot, got out and helped Po out, then offered Kate his arm.

Po looked over at Kate. "You look especially beautiful tonight."

"I second that. What Po said." P.J. smiled.

"It's the company. How could someone not feel special with one of you on either side of me?" She tucked an arm in each of theirs and they walked together toward the clubhouse.

Kate's dress flowed like liquid silk over her hips and down to her ankles. She laughed as she tripped slightly on the uneven bricks. "See? I don't have the genes for these crazy heels. Give me my Birkenstocks any day."

But even her husky laugh, slightly too loud and causing the couple in front of them to turn their heads and frown before continuing up the walk, was not enough to keep P.J. from sideways glances.

"My wonder woman," he said, looking into her eyes.

"One who makes you wonder?" Kate's asked. "That's a good thing."

Kate did just that, Po could see. She made the man beside her wonder about all sorts of things. Good things, probably tantalizing things.

But in between those more pleasurable thoughts, there was always that other wonder. Kate made P.J. wonder how he could keep her safe.

And that was the thought that kept Po—who had promised Kate's mother that she would be safe—awake at night.

Phoebe and Jimmy Mellon were at the door waiting for them when the threesome walked beneath the canopy and up the wide fan of steps.

"This is the happiest day of my life," Phoebe declared, hugging them all. "I get to sit with my best friends at this club that I usually dread going to more than my annual ob-gyn checkup." She hugged Kate and Po, then gave P.J. a kiss on the cheek. "I love you, P.J.," she said between giggles.

"One glass of wine and all Phoebe's filters dissolve into nothingness," Jimmy said, laughing and hugging his wife. "But come on in, folks. I echo Phoebe's sentiment, except for that bit about the ob-gyn."

Inside, all was light and airy, and a festive mood drew the crowd through the wide hallways and into the rooms in the back. French doors opened to the terrace, and people spilled outside to look at the moon and enjoy the warm spring air. Waiters and waitresses, carrying trays of wine and champagne, tiny stuffed mushrooms and plump oysters with lemon, wound their way in and out between happy groups of people.

"Your mother-in-law puts on a fancy gig, Phoebs," P.J. observed.

"I know. Can you imagine when the twins turn sixteen?" Phoebe's laughter circled the room and in minutes Eleanor, Maggie, Leah, and her husband, Tim, found the small group.

"Phoebe's laugh is better than a whistle," Leah said. "We just followed the ripples."

"Are Selma and Susan coming?" Po asked.

"They're sitting with the Elderberry merchants, but will join us later," Leah said.

A waiter appeared and passed out tall champagne flutes.

"Where is the quilt?" Eleanor asked. "The pièce de résistance?"

"Just follow me, folks." Phoebe spun around on her three-inch heels and led them through the crowd and an archway to the room beyond. There on the wall was Jacques's donation to the evening, with tiny lights reflecting off the gold thread that outlined Esther Woods's bird.

"It looks even more beautiful than I remembered," Kate said softly.

Po stood in front of it, staring up at the amazing design, the flowing curves quilted in pale yellows and golds. And the magnificent bird in the center. It looked so free, she thought, and thought about Esther's daughter. Perhaps she was finally free as well.

Her eyes took in every detail, the border of deep gold fabric, quilted in swirls that mirrored the wings of the bird. Laurel had cared for the quilt like a child, Jacques had said. Mending torn threads, treating it like a child, he said once.

Po looked at the border on the bottom and imagined Laurel mending it carefully. A labor of love, she thought. Perhaps to be closer to her mother. The quilt looked to be in excellent condition now, without frays or loose threads. But maybe just touching it brought back the few good memories Laurel had when she was with her mother, when she was Ann Woods.

"It is beautiful, non?"

Po turned around and looked into the pensive face of Jacques. "It is beautiful." She hugged him and together they looked up at the quilt as if they were standing in the Louvre, looking up at the Mona Lisa.

"I think this is a kind, generous thing you are doing," Po said.

Before Jacques could respond, Bill McKay came up beside them.

"Jacques," Bill said, resting a hand on his shoulder. "What a generous gift."

Po stepped back. Bill was dressed in a fine Italian suit, looking every bit the wealthy real estate magnate and future politician. His shoulders were broad like a quarterback's, his stance confident and tall.

"You like it, Bill?" Jacques asked.

"It's a wonderful gift. And I for one will make sure it brings in a pretty penny for the SafeHome we're building."

"The auction will be soon?"

"Janna tells me it's after the buffet. After everyone has had a couple glasses of wine." He smiled at Jacques. "That's when everyone gets generous."

* * * *

The buffet was a glorious affair, and Po almost forgot the heaviness in her heart. After dinner, a dessert bar drew folks back to their feet and they mingled with plates of chocolate-covered strawberries and crème brûlée in their hands, while a harpist played in the background and waiters cleared the tables, preparing for the auction. A dozen or so other gifts—vacations in Colorado, gold chandelier earrings, paintings, memberships to a health club—would be auctioned first, and then Jacques's quilt.

"You could almost forget we're living under this pall of murder, couldn't you?" Maggie said.

Po nodded. "It's good to see Jacques smile. If not for that, I don't think I could have come."

Kate walked over, balancing three glasses of wine in her hands. She handed two of them over and they walked onto the terrace together, away from the crowd surrounding Jacques's quilt, exclaiming over it, coaxing the person next to them to prepare their bid. In the distance, they could hear the river moving in the black night. "Laurel's body was found just a little south of here," Maggie said.

Kate nodded. "I wonder how long it will take for us to look at the river and not think of her, floating all the way from the bridge."

Po put her hands on the railing, looking out into the darkness, half-listening to the conversation. She took a sip of wine, and then put it back down, her mind turning back to Kate's comment. "Kate," she said abruptly, "what did you just say?"

"I said the river makes us think of Laurel."

"No, about where she was thrown in the river." Po's heart skipped a beat.

"Oh, you know—that spot near the bridge where the incline is filled with brambles. It's far from where she was found. I remember you and Mom never wanted us to play down there. It was secluded, kind of scary. It must be a couple miles from where she was found, don't you think?"

"How did you know where she was thrown into the river? Did P.J. tell you?"

"Did I tell her what?" P.J. walked up behind them.

"I wondered how Kate knew where Laurel was thrown into the river." Po tried to keep her voice steady, but the events of the last few days were crowding down on her, squeezing the air out of her lungs.

P.J. frowned. "No. I didn't tell Kate that. That information hasn't been released."

Kate looked from Po to P.J. She frowned. "But I heard someone mention where she was thrown into the river."

"Who told you, Kate?" Po asked. Her body tensed.

Kate set her wine glass on the terrace wall. She racked her brain. It shouldn't be difficult to remember—she didn't talk to many people about this. Finally she shook her head. "Sorry, Po, I can't remember. But give me time."

"It might be important, Kate," P.J. said.

"I think it is important, P.J.," Po said quietly. "You and I need to have a talk."

The tingle of a bell announced the beginning of the auction and slowly the crowd began gathering in the auction salon, coffee cups and wine glasses in hand. P.J. looked over at Po as they started inside. He lifted his brows.

"It can wait, P.J.," she said over the crowd. But not for long, she thought.

Janna and Bill stood in front of the room with Meredith Mellon, quieting the crowd and announcing the beginning of the auction. The roomful of people clapped hard in appreciation for the work of the chairpersons, and the auctioneer climbed up to a podium to begin the show.

Po stood in the back, looking across the crowd. Max Elliott caught her eye. He lifted a hand in a wave, then wove his way to her side. "Po," he whispered. "There's something I want to talk to you about."

Po nodded, and they walked back to the terrace door. "We can see when the quilt auction begins from here," she whispered, then turned her back to the room and looked at Max. "There's something I want to talk to you about, too. You're on the board of United Quarry, am I right?"

He nodded. "You're a step ahead, as always. I've toyed with breaching client confidentiality, but I ran into Kate today and she told me you were looking up old newspaper articles at the library. I knew you'd come across it."

"Did you know the Woodses, Max?"

Max paused for a long time, and Po wasn't sure he was going to answer her. But it didn't matter now. She knew the answer.

"I knew them in a way," Max said finally. "Al worked for United Quarry. And the company helped him out when he had some personal problems. I handled their checks back then."

"Helped him out how?"

"Gave out money when needed. I didn't know what it was for. That wasn't my job. But Al Woods had problems, and for some reason, United Quarry was helping him out."

"So they gave extra money to Al Woods? Why?"

Max shrugged. "I didn't know then. Or maybe I didn't want to know. I sent money where I was told to send it. For a long time I sent it to a place in New York, to some woman, to pay for things."

"Ann's aunt."

Max nodded. "I suppose. One of my board functions was to handle special funds, and that's where the money came from. And it went wherever I was told to send it."

"Generous company," Po said.

Max heard the sharp edge to Po's voice. He nodded. "More than that. Al got a big raise and a bonus so he could buy a big house. It was odd, made lots of people mad as hell. Al Woods was a drunken bum, and he was treated like a king. Briefly, anyway. No one really mourned when his truck ran off the road that night. No one cared. The company seemed to. They buried the Woodses in fine manner and that was that, the end of a chapter."

"Except for a teenage daughter left in New York."

"Right. But she was better off, Po. You didn't know the dad. He was a real mess. But I had trouble with the use of those discretionary funds, the movement of money between the companies owned by the same group, lots of things. So I quit the board and moved on. And I swear I didn't know until recent days what the connection was. But I sure as hell now know why Laurel St. Pierre hated me. She got those checks, saw my name. I was responsible—"

A movement from inside caught their attention and the lights dimmed briefly, announcing the auction of Jacques's quilt.

"We need to be in there for this," Po said. "But Max, I think I know why Laurel St. Pierre was murdered."

Max stared at her, but before he could pursue her comment, Po had disappeared inside the room. She stood in the back row, watching hands begin to rise as the auctioneer announced the minimum bid. Max stood in the shadows near the terrace, watching her.

"I have $800," the auctioneer called out in his unique staccato beat.

The room was packed, and all eyes were on the auctioneer as two men stood slightly in front of him, noting the raised hands.

Po heard a familiar voice in front. Bill McKay was bidding on the quilt, keeping his promise to Jacques to raise the ante. Po could see him near the front, Janna pressed closely into his side. They were smiling broadly, and Po noticed several flash bulbs go off.

Another bid came from the right, and a hand answered from a few rows behind. Po stared at the quilt, still lit with the tiny lights, showing the amazing craftsmanship of a woman who had so little else in her life, who created this amazing work of art.

Again, the bid was countered, and Po watched in fascination as it bounced back and forth between an art dealer in the back of the room and a stranger up in the front. Po didn't recognize him, but Max whispered that he was with United Quarry, a board member who had been there when Max was on the board. A close advisor to the owner. *The owner.* Of course.

Po stared at the man and watched as the gallery owner responded. She strained to see if the man in the front was bidding on his own. A turn of the man's gray head, a nod in the direction of the audience, was all Po needed to see.

The click in Po's head was so loud she was sure the whole room must have heard it.

The care Laurel had given to the quilt.

The break-in at Jacques's lovely home, looking for something, something Laurel had left behind.

The few missing pieces to the puzzle.

And without a second thought, Po stepped forward, out of the shadows, and in a loud clear voice, joined the bidding. Several heads turned to hear who had challenged the two men, but the gallery owner immediately answered Po's bid, and heads quickly turned back to the auctioneer. A rush of excitement ran through the crowd as they felt the thrill of the chase. When the man from United Quarry countered the bid, Po had had enough. She needed to stop this. The bidding was up to six thousand dollars. Po took a deep breath. Sorry, Scott, she murmured. I know you don't like frivolous spending, but it's for a very good cause, believe me.

Po cleared her throat, and in a loud voice, bid $12,000 on Esther Woods's bird quilt.

A chain of oohs and aahs passed through the crowd like the wave at a baseball game. Then a lone individual started clapping, and in seconds the entire room burst into a noisy show of appreciation for Po's generous gift. To outbid her, should anyone be so inclined, would be an embarrassment. And the gesture would draw unfortunate attention to the bidder. Po smiled and ignored the frantic beating of her heart.

She'd won.

Chapter 27

Bill McKay, with Janna at his side, concluded the auction with a gracious thanks to Jacques St. Pierre for the gift of his quilt, and an equal thanks to the winner of the evening's auction, Mrs. Portia Paltrow.

The crowd loved it all, the competition, the cause, the food and the wine and the invitation to move into the other room, where there'd be dancing and music.

"Po!" Kate said, weaving her way through the crowd to Po's side. "I can't believe it. You have Laurel's quilt. I had no idea you were going to do this."

Po smiled, but she could hardly find her voice. And she surely couldn't admit that she had had no earthly intention of spending a small fortune on a quilt when she walked through the door three hours ago. She took a deep breath to ward off the wave of exhaustion that pressed down on her. Max brought her a glass of water and she nodded in gratitude. She drained the glass.

"Po, are you all right?" Kate asked.

"I'm fine, sweetie," Po said. "Tired, is all. I've never won an auction before."

"Would you like us to take you home?"

"No, you go dance. You've got to dance with the one who brung you, didn't you know?"

"Of course I know. You and mom used to recite that silly ditty to me before every dance I ever went to."

"Well, then let's do it," P.J. said, cupping her elbow in the palm of his hand. "Po, you sit, we'll dance. Max, you keep an eye on Po. I don't trust her these days." He nodded at Max, then swept Kate onto the dance floor and out of their sight.

As Kate and P.J. disappeared in the swirl of moving bodies, Bill walked up, his arm outstretched to shake Po's hand. "Congratulations, milady. You've got yourself a magnificent quilt, and the SafeHome fund has a generous contribution."

"Thank you, Billy," Po said.

"You look a little tired." He looked around and focused on Max, "Max? Want to give this generous lady a ride home?"

Po interrupted. "I'm not ready just yet, Billy, I'd like to collect my quilt first. I believe the ladies are taking it down."

"It may take a while, Po. I hear it took them all afternoon to put it up after Jacques dropped it off. I'll have a couple of the fellows help me fold and wrap it, and I'll drop it off myself tomorrow."

Meredith Mellon squeezed her beaded body in front of Bill and gave Po a hug. "You are wonderful, Po," she said. "What a nice gift." She turned toward Bill. "And as for you, sir, you are wanted in the lobby. There's a photographer waiting to take a picture of you and Janna for Kansas City's *Independent.*"

Bill looked at Po, then glanced over toward the lobby where the photographer hovered over his pile of equipment. Janna stood next to him, waiting for Bill. "Po, you'll be okay?" he asked. "I'll be back in a minute."

"Come, Bill. This is important for your campaign," Meredith instructed, and she took him by the arm, leading him away.

"Max," Po said abruptly. "Would you please take me home?"

But first she summoned Leah's husband to help Max get the quilt down, folded, and placed in the back of Max's Pathfinder.

"Did you tell Kate you were leaving, Po?" Max asked, opening the car door for her. "Won't she worry?"

Po frowned. She should have told Kate before she went back onto the dance floor. But she'd let Phoebe know, so the word would pass to Kate, and she would know Po was fine. It was a good moment to sneak out without causing commotion, and Po didn't want to draw attention to herself. She just wanted to be home. Home with her quilt. She needed to know she was right before she called in the police and ruined a person's life.

* * * *

Kate stood on the side porch of the club, watching Max's car race off into the night. She'd left P.J. alone on the dance floor, rushing to find Po. She had finally remembered who told her where Laurel St. Pierre was thrown into the Emerald River. She needed to tell Po—and she needed to tell her immediately.

* * * *

Po and Max drove down the curving drive, passing the railed fields where the horses grazed, and headed to the Endicott home. They drove in silence for several miles, crossing over the bridge where it had all begun, then through the sleeping Elderberry neighborhood.

"He was bidding for someone else," Max said finally. Although he was the one who spoke the words, they were pulled from Po's thoughts.

She nodded. "I could see the exchange, but only because I was looking for it."

"I should have seen everything, Po. Should have seen it years ago. The company was playing God, manipulating people's lives."

"It wasn't the company," Po said. "It was the man at the top. He held the strings, Max. People did what he wanted." Max turned into Po's driveway and pulled the car up to the back door. Without a word they got out of the car, opened the back of Max's SUV, and gently removed their precious cargo. Around them the night was still and black, the warm spring air and sweet smell of the lilac bushes masking the dread in Po's heart.

Po held the door open for Max, then switched on lights as Max carried the quilt over to the kitchen table.

"Max, I didn't mean to involve you in this—"

"I became involved when I sent money to Ann Woods's aunt in New York. I didn't realize until we put pieces together today that it was probably used for hospital bills for Ann, or whatever they arranged for her and the baby. But it doesn't matter. I was involved when the money from the foundation was used to buy Al Woods a house. It didn't make sense to a lot of us, but no one talked about it. No one knew, or if they did, they didn't say, that it was to cover up the family's sins. But we didn't know because we didn't ask or look or try to put it all together."

Po waved Max's words away and walked over to the quilt.

"Max, it's done. The important thing now is to prove it and not let any more lives be torn apart in the process. And I think Laurel's quilt holds the answer. Jacques told me this was Laurel's child, the one she could never have. Her life, he said. I think Jacques meant those words far more literally than he even knew. Laurel was blackmailing people, or at the least, holding information that would ruin their lives. Max, if I'm right, this quilt is the key to Laurel's life—and to her death."

Gently, as if rubbing a baby's back, Po stretched the quilt out on the table and padded around the edges.

Esther had used a thick batting for the interlining and Po couldn't feel any bumps in it. Her heart was tight in her chest. Somehow, she knew the quilt had to be the answer. And if they couldn't find it, a murderer would go free. She lifted the edge of the quilt and looked at the double binding Esther had used to finish the edges, making them strong, less likely to tear or come apart. And then Po saw it. The careful disruption of the quilting pattern, the new threads that held the binding on. The fabric was slightly darker along a portion of the edge, probably oil from Laurel's hands as she sat with the quilt, pulling it apart, and burying her life inside of it.

Po took a pair of scissors from the kitchen drawer and began snipping the newer stitches that Laurel had applied to the backing. She must have done this many times, Po thought. Carefully, she smoothed the binding flat against the table, sliding her fingers beneath the double layer of batting. Her fingers slipped in easily and immediately touched up against stiff paper. Slowly Po pulled out an envelope buried between the layers of fill. She reached in again and found three more pieces of paper hidden in Laurel's quilt.

Max watched in silence as Po pulled the envelopes from the quilt. "How did you know, Po?"

"It was Jacques. He told me Laurel used to take the quilt down all the time to repair it and dust it. When I looked at it more closely, I realized it wouldn't have needed that kind of repair. Esther was a master seamstress and quilter. She used double binding on this quilt and strong quilting thread. Hanging on a wall wouldn't cause it to fall apart. Laurel was doing something else with it.

"And then there was the break-in at Jacques's. Why would anyone break into his house and not take some of the lovely things Laurel had purchased? He or she was looking for something, and they didn't find it. There had to be something there that Laurel had hidden and someone wanted. What better place to hide the secrets of her life than in her mother's quilt?"

The envelopes weren't sealed, and Po pulled a yellowed photograph out of the first one. She held it up to the light and recognized Esther Woods. She was sitting on a couch with her arms wrapped around a little girl at her side. It was Laurel and her mother, in maybe one of the few peaceful moments of their lives. The second envelope was bigger and held a check for $50,000 made out to Ann Woods from United Quarry and never cashed.

Beside her, Max recognized his own signature and stiffened.

Ann's payoff, Po thought. *Have your baby and stay out of our lives.* And he'd made sure she couldn't come back home—Al Woods wouldn't allow it now. The last envelope had legal papers—a medical report, and a birth certificate and death certificate, all in one package. It was for Ann's baby, born too early and with too much trauma to make it in life. And a medical record detailing the damage to her body that would prevent more pregnancies. Po put on her glasses and read the fine print on the birth certificate. Ann Woods was listed as the mother, and, as Po had suspected, probably for days now, the father was someone they all knew. Listed without his permission. Without his knowledge. But listed by the one woman who knew with certainty who the father was.

The high school football player with whom Ann had fallen in love. And who had gotten her pregnant and then threw her away.

Max shook his head. "You're smarter than I am, Po."

The familiar creak of Po's door took their attention away from the quilt. Po and Max spun around and stared at Bill McKay.

He'd come in the front door, still elegant in his Italian suit, and stood just inside the dark hallway, staring at the two figures standing over the quilt. At his side, but one step ahead, was Kate.

Po's breath caught in her throat. Her eyes were riveted to the gun pressed tightly into Kate's back.

"Bill—" Po began. She took a step toward Kate, her arms reaching out to her.

"Back up," Bill said.

His voice was eerily calm. He could have been addressing his campaign or the weather or a new book they'd all read.

Bill looked sideways at Kate. "Pretty Kate should have minded her own business. I was parked a few houses down, near the house I grew up in—remember, Po? —when I saw Katie here headed for your back door."

Bill moved closer to the table, pushing Kate along with him and urging Max and Po to step back. He stared down at the photograph and papers spread across the top of the quilt. The birth certificate was in the center and his name popped up off the bottom of the page. Bill turned white.

"What a fool she was," he said. "It was all a joke. The team dared me. They do it every year. Quarterback dare. But she wasn't supposed to get pregnant. Then she wanted me to marry her!" A harsh laugh followed, He shook his head and looked at Max and Po, as if they would shake their head and tsk at Ann Woods's foolishness. And then he added quietly, "I didn't even know her real name. Carrie. That's what we all called her. The scary, crazy girl from that old movie."

Beside him Kate's blood churned and her face turned bright red with anger. Po felt her boiling anger and prayed she wouldn't do anything foolish.

"That's why you'd never eat at Jacques's while she was there," Po said calmly, trying to lessen the electricity in the room.

Bill nodded. "I knew she was here—she called me once and told me who she was, that she'd lost the kid. Then she told me she thought the whole town would be interested in the story, and she had all the pieces she needed to make it believable."

"I suppose this wasn't as easy to clean up as when your father neatly sent Ann away and paid off Al Woods," Po said. She suspected strongly that the drunken crash that took Ann's parents to their death was far more than that. Brakes had probably been tampered with, and Al and Esther died in a very convenient accident. It would never be proven now, but the tragedy of Laurel's death could be.

"I knew Jackson McKay owned several companies," Po continued, always keeping Kate in the corner of her eye, as if seeing her there would keep her safe. Talking to Bill seemed to calm him some, so she continued, her heart wedged painfully in her chest. "But it wasn't until I read the accounts of the accident, then probed a little deeper into United Quarry, that I realized Jackson was the CEO."

"My dad was a genius at keeping things in separate compartments, even me. But he was never mayor." Bill thought he heard a noise and glanced toward the back door, then back to Po and Max. He nodded toward the door. "My car is down the street, but we'll use yours, Max. Better to destroy a Chevy. It's good you're here in one package. Maybe once the three of you are gone, this can end. It would have all been okay, you know, if she hadn't come back. Couldn't leave it alone. She was going to package it all up, then send it all to the newspaper and television stations. It'd be a great news item in Kansas City, too, she said.

"Foolish, horrible twit."

He looked at Po calmly and for a minute Po held out hope he had had a change of heart and realized the foolishness of what he was doing. That he would never get away with it. Jackson McKay had bred an arrogance in his son that defied reason.

But then Billy said, "My father's not the only one who can plan, you see. It's all set up for me now. Janna's father will invest in my ventures. I'll be a successful businessman. Then mayor. They like me, you know, all these people in Crestwood. Even Jacques likes me. My life will be bigger than Jackson T. McKay ever dreamed of."

The bitterness in his voice startled Po for a minute. "Billy, I don't think you want to harm more people. This doesn't help you get back at your dad. Maybe you didn't even mean to harm Laurel."

Kate moved slightly and Bill took her arm, pinching it slightly. He looked at Po. "I thought I could talk to her. But she didn't want to talk—she wanted to ruin me, and she wouldn't back down. She wouldn't listen." His voice trailed off as if his mind was going in different directions at once. The carefully held together Bill McKay was unraveling. "Janna—she's a bright girl, a little drab, sure. Her family situation more than makes up for that. But she's like all women—too nosey and manipulating—and she almost ruined it. She thought I was meeting a woman that night and she was jealous. So she followed me and hid in the bushes. She knew it all. Knew the wine guy was blackmailing me. Knew how Laurel died—"

"And where," Kate said. "Janna was the one who mentioned where Laurel was killed, Po. I finally remembered."

"And the bleach on the quilt, that was Janna, wasn't it?" Po asked. "She couldn't bear the thought of losing you to prison. She wanted to protect you."

Bill shook his head. "That fat woman in the bakery told me about the bleach, and I knew immediately from the look on Janna's face that she had done it. I was furious. She could have ruined everything. She knew you were all prying into this and thought a warning would scare you off."

Kate's brows pulled together when Billy pushed the metal more forcefully into her shoulder blades, but it didn't stop her from talking. "Janna hung around us enough to know that we were getting closer. Listening in on our conversations in Selma's shop. She'd have given her life to protect the only man who had ever paid any attention to her. And you would have let her."

"She's smart but she doesn't think logically."

"She loves you, Billy. And now you're ruining her life, too," Kate said.

"Stop—all of you. Let me think." He rubbed his temples and looked around the room, like a kid looking for a place to hide. Then he backed up toward the door, his gun still pressed into Kate's side.

"We'll go to the quarry," he said at last. "That's where I met Jason Sands that night. He laughed lightly. "Now why did Laurel confide in that useless guy? The jerk thought he could milk me dry. She wasn't very good at picking her men, was she? I planned on having the company fill the quarry in—for safety, you know." He laughed lightly. "But I wasn't fast enough. This time I will be. Come, friends, let's go."

"I don't think so, Billy."

Before Bill McKay could register that the voice was directly behind him, P.J. knocked the gun to the floor, twisted Billy's arm in a painful grip, and shoved him into the hands of half the Crestwood police force, waiting with open arms on the front steps.

"Po, you've got to start locking your doors," P.J. muttered, and then he filled his arms with the woman who had disappeared from the dance floor an hour before and never returned. "You're supposed to dance with the one who brung you," he whispered into her neck. "Not run off with the quarterback."

Po watched the two of them as she wiped the tears from her eyes, her heart still pounding as the sirens and cars started up and tore down the street. *Oh, Liz,* Po moaned softly. *That was surely a close one. I'll do better next time.*

Epilogue

It was bouillabaisse, of course, that was featured at the unveiling of Jacques's quilt. And a fine arugula salad, with greens from the new organic farm that Jacques had discovered just south of town. He'd baked the baguettes that morning and whipped up bowls of butter with snips of rosemary tossed in for color and flavor. The place was closed to the public for the evening, and only special friends filled the small restaurant.

A warm breeze wrapped the space with the smells of May—lilac and tulips, violets and pansies. Beside the restaurant, flowering crab apple trees and pink dogwoods, lit from beneath with tiny lights, welcomed the guests. It was a Kansas spring in all its glory.

All of the quilters were there, having worked feverishly all month to finish the quilt. Max Elliott came, and the whole street of Elderberry merchants and spouses. Ambrose and Jesse provided the champagne, and Randy Haynes played his guitar in the background. When Jacques pulled the sheet down and revealed the French Quarter quilt, its boiling pot a shiny blue-black image at the bottom, and the brilliant, colorful fish soaring across the pieced background, there wasn't a dry eye in the room.

"It is perfect," Jacques declared, lifting his glass of champagne. "And you are friends like no others."

The toasts echoed around the room, cheers and hoots and sighs of relief.

Janna Hathaway had disappeared from town, scooped up by another domineering father. Selma wasn't going to press charges for the damaged quilt—it was such a minor thing, done out of fear for a man not worthy of her love. And Janna had suffered tremendously in the process.

Billy had felt nothing for Janna, the quilters had conjectured. She was a stepping-stone for him. And that was just another sad, cruel piece of the whole horrible story.

"Po, what will you do with your quilt?" Jacques asked as the happy crowd milled around them.

"A perfect solution, Jacques. The one good thing to come out of all of this is SafeHome. They made a hunk of money at the gala, and donations are still coming in, so building the home will become a reality. Meredith Mellon has taken over the whole project, so you know it will happen. I suggested she call it Laurel's Place—and the quilt will hang in the entry."

Jacques leaned over and kissed her on the cheek. Tears welled in his eyes, but his face was full of happiness. Waiters appeared then, as if by magic, carrying colorful bowls heaped full of steaming bouillabaisse, and people moved toward the white-clothed tables.

"Where's Kate?" Po asked as Max took her elbow and directed her to a table by the window. Kate had had nightmares following Bill McKay's arrest, and she was filled with an anger that Po knew would take her a while to shake. But as Kate would do, she was purging it in an appropriate way—using her photography class to focus on images of strong women, women taking charge of their lives. They'd have a show at the end of summer and sell the framed photos to benefit Laurel's Place.

P.J. had found it difficult to be apart from Kate for more than a few minutes at a time after the events of the past weeks. Po knew that she would no longer be the only one looking out for her best friend's daughter. Kate would resist, of course, but it wouldn't matter.

"I saw her near the kitchen door earlier," Phoebe said, as she scooped Emma up in her arms. Jimmy followed close behind with little Jude toddling beside him.

Po smiled at the twins, then moved around the room, searching for a glimpse of the bright red blouse Kate was wearing that night. As she wove her way toward the back of the restaurant, a flash of red through a rear window caught her eye. Po walked over to the back door and looked out into the dark night.

"Kate?" she called softly.

There was no answer, and Po stood there for a minute, her eyes adjusting to the darkness. And then a sound drew her eyes to the flowering crab that Jacques had planted out in the alley. A touch of beauty, he called it.

And then she spotted movement, and two figures beneath the branches of the tree materialized, unaware of Po—or anything else, it seemed to her.

She stood there for just a brief moment, watching P.J. and Kate. They were wrapped in one another's arms, shadowed from moonlight by the branches of the tree. The nightmares would soon stop for Kate, Po thought, and she nodded at the sight that filled her heart to overflowing.

I told you it would be okay, Liz, she whispered to her best friend. *Have I ever let you down?*

And with a lighter step, Po joined her friends inside over heaping bowls of bouillabaisse, some laughter, and bonds of friendship deepening and lighting the small restaurant from within.

Printed in the United States
by Baker & Taylor Publisher Services